WILLIAM BOONE

THE

CARTEL

AFFAIR

D1518189

William E. Boone

Snipers Roost Press supports the right to free expression and the value of copyright. The purpose of copyright is to encourage writers and artist to produce creative works that enrich our culture.

The scanning, uploading and distribution of this book without permission is theft of the author's intellectual property. If you would like permission to use material from this book (other than for review purposes), please contact:

william@williameboone.com.

Thank you for your support of the author's rights.

Travis Bones is a trademark of William E. Boone.

Snipers Roost Press provides William E. Boone for speaking events. To find out more, go to: www.williameboone.com.

Library of Congress Control Number:
2020920572

ISBN: 978-1-6913-4149-8

Copyright ©2020 by William Boone

Printed in the United States of America.

The Cartel Affair

To Donna Boone

TRACY,

THANKS SO MUCH FOR
THE LOVE AND SUPPORT.!!
I HOPE YOU ENJOY THE
BOOK.

Love,

William Boone

ACKNOWLEDGEMENTS

First and foremost, I wish to dedicate this book to my beautiful and loving wife Donna Matthews Boone. Without her, none of this would be possible. She supports and believes in me when no one else will. For this I'm eternally grateful. Without her help this work may never have happened and certainly would not be as successful as it is.

I also wish to thank Rebecca Wilkinson for being my final editor and the input she has given me on this project. Without her professionalism and guidance this project would not be happening. She went far and above what was asked of her, and for this I am eternally grateful.

Special thanks go out to my bosses Skeet Hartis and Jerry Longfellow for allowing me to research and do some writing while working for them. Without this time, this project would still be in the planning stages. Thank you for your support and happy reading

.

PRELUDE

Travis Bones has spent the last three months in the jungle following his target, learning his habits, and the how and where of his operations. He has watched as his savages took over entire villages and forced men, women and children to work for his operation. He has witnessed the brutality and unspeakable acts his animals forced upon the villagers. On a few occasions, he has intervened to stop the torture and killing his ruthless men perpetuate. Travis has killed over 50 of his men. The cartel knows someone is out there causing problems but isn't sure who it is. Or so Travis thought. Travis has destroyed over a dozen working drug manufacturing operations in the three months he has been in country. The cartel leaders are growing increasingly frustrated with this interference. Travis has had a few close calls but has managed to stay one step ahead of their men. Travis has finally gathered the information he needs to finalize his last mission as a sniper for the Marine Corps. It's time to eliminate the target.

ONE

Medellin, Antioquia, Colombia

It seemed like he had been on this roof forever, but it had only been four days in the hot sun waiting for that perfect moment to take what he hoped was his last shot. Travis had been following and learning the routines of his target for over three months.

"It's 12:14. In one minute his car will pull up to take him to lunch. That leaves me 45 minutes of clear time inside the house before the housekeeper gets back from the market to start preparing dinner."

Travis slowly makes his way over to the ladder on the back wall that leads to the ground and descends to the street below. He slowly comes up the alley between the buildings and waits until he sees his car pull out of the drive. He crosses the street, and follows the wall around the front of the house until he gets to where the bushes in the yard can hide him as he crosses the top of the fence. Travis then follows the bushes around until he's out of sight of the guard house on the other side. Travis enters the house through the door to the cook's quarters. There is no camera on this doorway.

Once inside, he quickly makes his way over to the control panel in the closet in the cook's room. The alarm is already off. The guard will be coming through in about 30 seconds to do his hourly check of the main house. It's now 12:29.

"How many times do I have to wait for this moron to walk through and stick his head in the cook's room to make sure the boogey man isn't in there? If he only knew just how close the boogey man really is to him he would shit his pants. Damn I'd love to see his expression if I jumped out of the closet and said boo. Whoops!!!!! Better be quiet, I hear dumb ass coming! And....... he's gone, time to go to work."

The first thing is to override the security system that dumb ass reset when he left. Done. Next is to link in the static loop to the security cameras. Done.

"Let's check my time. 12:34. That leaves me 24 minutes to get everything done before the cook gets back. Better hurry!"

"Ok, let's get the charge shaped and put on the gas line for the stove in the kitchen. This will cover the sound of the shot later. Just have to make sure the signal can reach from the roof across the street. Should be good. Now to set the charge in his bedroom upstairs. I'll place it under the bed and face it toward the balcony doors. This will cover him in debris and give me more time to make my escape after the shot. Now to get downstairs and set the charge on the gas tank outside the house. This tank faces the guard barracks. If I set the charge on the back side of the tank out of sight, then the blast and shrapnel from the tank should cover the only doorway in the guard barracks. This will take out anyone coming out of the barracks in response to the blast in the house. Ok. Time check. It's 12:58. Time to take the loop off the cameras and reset the alarm. I'll stay in the bushes until the cook gets inside and then go over the wall. Here she comes, right on time. 13:00 on the nose. If nothing else she's dependable. Good. She's inside, the alarm's off. Time to go."

Safely back on the roof, now Travis will hunker down, review the mission plan, and reflect on his future.

"Time check. 13:22. The target's at lunch with his U.S. connection, Senator William Baker, a member of the Armed Services Committee. That's why I have been black for over four months."

With connections like this the target could easily be warned about any movement against him.

How did Gabriel Escobar get to where he is, you ask? Who's Gabriel Escobar? The last name Escobar speaks for itself when it comes to abuse and drugs. Yes, he's part of that Escobar clan. He is a trusted member and leader in the Medellin Cartel and is known in this part of Columbia for his merciless and ruthless endeavors when dealing with problems. It's highly suspected that he's the illegitimate son of Pablo Escobar, the head of the Medellin Cartel. However, the age just doesn't work for Travis. Gabriel is 19 years old. Pablo is only 29. Exactly how he's related may never be known. Especially after this evening is over.

"Excuse me as I digress." Back to going over the plan.

Gabriel will arrive home around 16:30 after his meeting is finished and he sees his mistress in town. He'll take a shower to, as he puts it; get the stench of his whore off of him. He'll eat at 17:30. At 18:00, he'll meet with the second in charge of his personal security force. Normally he meets with the head of security, but he's with Gabriel's wife in Jamaica on vacation. Gabriel is supposed to meet her there tomorrow. Travis doesn't think he'll make the plane. He stayed behind to have this meeting today. Travis didn't know for sure until today's meeting that William Baker was the contact. Travis knew it was someone high in the government, but he wasn't sure who. That's why only two people know where he is and who he's after. Major General Louis Stevens, Commander of the 1st Marine Division and Peter Turner, Director of the CIA. They would be happy to finally find out for sure who the contact was. Or so Travis thought at the time anyway.

At 18:30, Gabriel calls and talks to his wife. At 19:00, Gabriel reads and catches up on the news until 20:15. At 20:15, Gabriel steps out onto his balcony to have his evening cigar. At 20:16, Travis blows the gas line on the stove in the kitchen and takes his shot at the same time. Travis then blows the charge under his bed and the charge on the outside gas tank. At 20:17, Travis departs the roof and makes his way to the hotel where he has had a room for the last three months under an assumed name. Travis will stay in town for a couple of days laying low and make his way to the extraction point after contact with Turner to arrange extraction. Time to rest now. Time check 13:35.

"Time check 20:00."

The weapon of choice for Travis is a 700 Remington Rifle M40A1 with a McMillan fiberglass stock and 10x Unerti fixed power scope. Travis makes last minute checks of the weapon and makes final adjustments on the scope. He gets his stand in place to make his shot. He puts the stand back from the edge of roof, so no one sees the gun, the muzzle flash or Travis himself when the shot is taken.

"Time check 20:15."

Time to chamber the round. Take a deep breath and let it out slowly. Travis places the remote by his foot so he can step on the button at the same time he squeezes the trigger. He checks the sights. Travis lets out his breath and squeezes the trigger while stepping on the remote button. All Hell breaks loose and he watches for the guards rushing out of the guard house. They start charging out and Travis blows the gas tank. Guards and tank explode together. Travis blows the charge in his bedroom. Travis breaks down his weapon and stand. He heads to the back edge of the roof and makes his way down to the alley below. Making sure no one has seen him, he heads to the back door of the hotel having practiced this routine more times than he can count. Travis slips in and up to his room without being seen. He places his rifle in its hiding place and then runs downstairs to the lobby acting scared and surprised and asking what has happened. After a respectable amount of time he goes back upstairs to his room. Travis has an appointment with Jack Daniels and a hot tub of water.

"Damn this water feels good!! Nothing better than a good stiff drink and a long hot soak in the tub. Except the same thing at home with my wife and son. I'll be home soon, baby."

Time to get the satellite phone and call Turner and get the ball rolling to get home."

"Hello."

"This is Dragonslayer searching for a dragon to slay."

"Merlin says a town two days walks from you. You will find a dragon to slay at high noon."

"The beast will be slayed at noon two days hence."

Time to rest for now and get an early start tomorrow. Time to dream of home.

"Let's get everything ready for the trip. Break the gun down. Get ready for public travel."

TWO

The next day Travis catches the bus from Medellin to Barbosa and takes a walk in the Aburra Valley area.

"Thank God it's September and not July. Damn, it's still hot as Hell out here!!! Do they really think we're dumb enough not to know every other pineapple plant is really coca? Let's see, from here I need to go 30 clicks north west to reach the extraction point. Let's see if I can avoid the roaming guards and get out cleanly. Yeah, right!!! We're off to see the wizard, the wonderful wizard of Barbosa!! Think they'll mind if I pull some coca plants up along the way? HI HO HI HO, it's off to work I go. Damn, I've been in the jungle way too long. Keep focused, dipshit, or you won't get home. I have to stop pulling these plants and get a move on. Only gone three miles in two hours. Won't make my date if I keep this up. Awe well, fun while it lasted.

Oh shit, guards and they have seen me. Time to disappear. Have to make the tree line before they get close. I figure they're about a half mile away in a truck. The woods are about a quarter mile so that makes it about three minutes before they get to me. Should have time."

Travis gets hidden before the guards make it to the tree line. "If they look up it'll get ugly. If they don't, we're good." Luckily after about five minutes of looking around, they get back in the truck and drive to the other side of the tree line to try to catch him there. Time to go. Two miles north around the other end of the tree line and Travis should be clear.

"Well, how about that. They aren't as dumb as I thought they were. They left me a surprise. A really noticeable surprise, but a surprise, nonetheless. These guys are well armed and at least one of them has advanced training in booby traps. A grenade with a trip wire. Make that two trip wires. Tricky little devil put a secondary trip wire to try to catch me. I might enjoy going one on one with this guy, but alas, I don't have time. I'll hold on to the grenade though. Time to roll. Change of plans. Not going around, going to them. If I let them go, they spread the word and I don't make my ride home. They expect me to run and hide. Advantage me, let's go get them. Ghillie suit on and ready to roll."

"Twenty minutes later and I have them in sight. Three of them. One by the truck. One about 15 feet to my left and the other about 50 feet to my right. Take the left one first. Let's use a garrote on him. Back to the one on the right and break his neck. Put on the shirt and hat from this one and back out of the woods toward the one at the truck. Turn quickly and put my knife through his throat so he makes no sound like the others. Gather up weapons and take stock of what I have. Three AK-47's with six clips, 12 grenades, two 357's, two 45's with four clips, one 9 MM with two clips and a fifty-cal. machine gun with 1500 rounds. I'm ready to have fun. Let's check out the truck. Toyota with a half tank of gas. Best of all, a radio to monitor traffic in the area and avoid roadblocks. A map marking all the guard shacks and buildings. Found my roost for the night. Only about three clicks from my extraction point. Have to hide the truck for the night. They'll be looking for it after not hearing from the guards I took out. Park it about two clicks from my roost and rig it with some grenades. Time to rest and wait for the boom. Time check 21:00."

"Awakened by the explosion. Time check, 01:15. Chatter on the radio. From what I can make out, got two of them with the explosion. Sounds like the guard called in more guys. So much for sleeping anymore tonight."

"I have ten hours and 45 minutes before my ride home gets in. I have three clicks to get to the extraction point. Let's go play and have some fun. Time to break out Jamie and have some fun with these guys. Yes, my weapon has a name! It's named Jamie after my dad. It's strong, reliable and never lets me down. Just like my dad. Ok. Let's get a little closer and have a look. One guy so far is all I see. About 150 yards. One click up and two right. Squeeze the trigger and he's no longer a threat. I'll wait and see if anyone else shows up."

"Time check 01:37. Looks like two vehicles coming from opposite directions. First vehicle stops and two men get out. I take the driver out as soon as he exits the vehicle. Before the passenger can react, I chamber another round and drop him. The second vehicle is getting close. They must have seen what happened because they stop short before getting to the other vehicle. I sight the driver and deliver a round down range. Bingo. Driver down. The passenger panics and ducks down in the floorboard. Guess this will be a waiting game. I'm tired of waiting and need to get moving so I move around to where I'm facing the passenger side of the vehicle. I put two rounds through the passenger door to the floorboard area. He hollers and jerks his head up. Round down range and bingo. Target down. Time to clean up and roll out. Time check 01:49."

"After checking all targets and grenading the vehicles to put them out of service, I put Jamie away and head out to my extraction point. Time check 02:21."

Having reached his extraction point without any further problems, Travis settles down to wait for his ride and think about his wife and son waiting for him to get home to them for good this time.

Travis's wife's name is Sarah. She's a long-haired beauty from Texas who's strong willed and stubborn but loves with a ferocity Travis had never seen before or since. She's his rock and what keeps him sane while he does what he does. Without her, Hell, he didn't even want to think about that!! He knew he wouldn't be the man he is without her, that he knew for sure. Sarah had given him a son they named James Henry Bones after her father and his father. James after Travis's dad and Henry after Sarah's dad. They called him Jamie. Jamie was Travis's pride and joy and Travis would move the world and Hell to make sure his son was safe and healthy. He had cotton blonde hair and steely blue eyes like his father. That's one of the things that had attracted Sarah to Travis in the first place. Travis had brown hair now but had cotton blonde hair when he was young. Sarah said that he could melt your heart with just a glance of those eyes, but at the same time freeze your blood with a glance if angry.

Sarah knew he couldn't talk about what he did; she knew it was very dangerous. She knew he had to do some very dark things and was determined that she and Jamie would be the light at the end of the tunnel for him. Travis was eternally grateful to have that in his life. He felt blessed. Life was good for Travis.

He hears a helicopter. "Time check 11:58." Time had gotten away from Travis as he was daydreaming about home. He checks the sky and sees his ride home coming in. They land and he climbs aboard. They lift off and he's on his way.

"What's the plan?"

"We're taking you to the CV-63 Sir."

"The Kitty Hawk?"

"Yes, Sir."

We touch down on the deck and they escort me to the captain in his quarters.

"Sir, Sergeant Bones reporting, Sir."

"At ease Sergeant."

"Thank you, Sir."

"I don't know who you are, but my orders are to get you cleaned up and on a plane to 8th & I in DC as soon as possible for debriefing."

"Yes, Sir."

"You got 20 minutes to be ready for flight."

"Yes, Sir."

"Dismissed."

Twenty minutes later, Travis boarded a C-2 Greyhound headed for Andrews Air Force Base in DC.

THREE

Washington, DC

The plane touched down at Andrews at 14:15 EST on Thursday, September 18, 1980. It was drizzling rain and in the mid 80's. A car was waiting. Travis rode to 8th & I in silence.

General Stevens and Mr. Turner met Travis out front of the 8th & I Barracks.

"Good afternoon, General."

"At ease Travis. This will be an informal meeting."

"Thank you, General. Hello, Mr. Turner. Why are we at 8th & I?"

"We're meeting with the Commandant. He's very interested to find out who the U.S. connection is."

"You're all in for a mighty big surprise. I know I was."

Travis couldn't believe he was about to meet the Commandant of the Marine Corps. Holy shit!! Travis is going to meet Four Star General Robert H. Barnsworth!!

"Good afternoon, Sir."

"At ease, Sergeant Bones. This is an informal debrief and we are not standing on formality or tradition. I want everyone to be comfortable. I hear good things about you, Bones, and I think you've single handedly done more to set back the drug cartels than all the negotiations combined. Good job, son. We need more like you. Now, down to business. What have you got for us?"

"Well Sir, first off, thank you for being so kind. Now, what I'm going to tell you will change the political landscape for years to come. The U.S. connection for the Escobar / Medellin Cartel is Senator William Baker of the Armed Services Committee."

"Holy Shit!!"

"You're saying Bill Baker is the Medellin Cartel's government connection?"

"Yes Sir, that's what I'm saying."

"Makes sense. He has the connections needed to get what they want done."

"Peter, did y'all have him on the radar for this?"

"No Sir, we did not. His name never came up."

"What do you think he'll do when he finds out about Gabriel being killed?"

"I don't see him doing anything out of the ordinary to draw attention to himself."

"You know they'll push for information on who did the deed to Gabriel."

"The only people who know that info are in this room, right?"

"That's correct."

"Does he have connections at the CIA to get the info?"

"I don't believe he does, no."

"Excuse me Sir; you have a level one message."

"Thank you, Sergeant. Gentlemen, excuse me for a moment. I have to take this. This is General Barnsworth. Thank you for the information. Get the car and my plane ready. General Stevens, Director Turner, I need the room please. I'll get back to you in a moment. Sergeant Bones, stay."

"Yes, Sir. What's going on Sir?"

"I sent a security detail to your home yesterday as a precaution. They didn't check in this morning. We sent backup out. The first team was found dead and your wife and son are missing. They have locked the scene down until we get there. We'll find them Sergeant. Let's get ready to travel."

"Gentlemen, we're going to California. I'll explain more on the plane. My car is waiting."

FOUR

On Board the Flight to California

"Once I heard that Sergeant Bones had a contact name, I decided to place a security detail to his wife and son until he got home. They checked in at 03:00. Nothing after that. I sent a backup team in to check at 05:00. All members of the alpha team were found dead. The back up detail immediately locked down the scene and are waiting for us to arrive. Sergeant Bones, I know that I can't stop you from being in this investigation, so I'll see to it you have whatever you need and any personnel that you need. Just don't do anything rash without checking with General Stevens first. Director Turner, he is to have any resources or assets he may need from you without any restrictions, clear?"

"Yes Sir, General. He will have my full cooperation."

"What do you need from us first?"

"I need to know what the comings and goings of Senator Baker have been for the last week. I need to know any and all property owned by him and his family or his wife's family. Where is he and are any of his properties showing any signs of activity? Who are his lobbyists? I want to know where he lives and if he's in DC right now or not. Whoever did this is trained. They took out a trained security detail. How many guys on the detail?"

"I believe there were four on the detail. Why does that matter?"

"It will tell me how many were on the crew and how well trained they were. If it was a four-man team on the security detail, they would have one out front, one in the back, one inside and one in the alley behind the house. Probably a three-man team that came for my family. They would strike at the same time in the front, rear and alley. Then they go inside, one takes out security while the other two grab my wife and son. Clean, quick and precise. Standard snatch and grab scenario. Sounds like military or law enforcement training. Probably hired guns that work as a team. Need to check that angle and see if anything or anyone stands out. Check financials for Senator Baker and see if he received or put out a large sum of money lately. We'll be landing at Pendleton soon. Director Turner, get started gathering info. General Stevens, if you'll get me the names of the security team that were killed, I would like to inform the families personally as soon as I'm done at the house. I would like to thank everyone in advance for their help and cooperation. Once we land things will move at a very fast pace and I'll be extremely busy. Again, thank you."

FIVE

Oceanside, California

"Boots on the ground people! General Barnsworth, I'd like for you to accompany me to the house. General Stevens and Director Turner, I need the info I requested as soon as humanly possible. I need the local and state police out of the way until I process the house. Sorry General Barnsworth, I don't mean to step on your toes or overstep my bounds, Sir."

"You're fine, son. I can't think of anyone better to lead this investigation than you. Just don't let it get to you or make you lose your professionalism."

"Yes, Sir. To tell you the truth Sir, it already has gotten to me, but that just drives me to work harder and faster to find my family!! Sir, I'll do whatever it takes to find them, Sir."

"I know son, I know. That's what I'm counting on."

"Thank you, Sir. That means a lot coming from you, Sir. Let's roll people!!!"

"I looked forward to getting home and seeing the house and hugging my family for so long, and now I can't because of some loose-lipped son of a bitch. Whoever is responsible for this will answer to me first and the courts second, Sir!"

"I don't want you doing anything on impulse, son, that you'll regret later. Believe me son, after what you've done for your country, no one wants to see them punished more than I do. I'll be personally involved in their case and will see justice done, no matter who they are or how well connected they may be."

"Let's take a look at the alley first. I want to get these boys off the scene and to their families as quickly as possible. They gave up their lives for me and my family and I don't take that lightly, Sir. I need justice for them and my family."

"We'll get them out as soon as you say."

"The body is positioned with his back to the wall of the backyard and his throat is cut. The perp must have come from the neighbor's yard across the side wall and over the top to cut his throat. He's well trained and probably military or government training in black ops. He would have had to come through all the yards from the end of the block to keep from being seen. Have all the neighbors questioned to see if any heard or saw anything. My bet is they didn't but check anyway. The guard on the backdoor is shot twice in the head. I'd say, judging from the blood spatter, one shot from the wall and the second shot standing over the body. Check the yards on both sides for brass, but my guess is you won't find any.

Judging from the size of the bullet holes, I'd say a 22 pistol, probably a Luger with a silencer. That's why no shots were reported. Two came over the wall in the back and the other came around the front. My guess is the guard out front will be shot the same way. Let's go find out."

"Just as I thought, same caliber. Judging from the blood spatter, the first shot came from the bushes on the right side and the second shot while standing over the body. This is a very personal and malicious killing. They meant for it to be ugly to leave a message! Let's check inside. The guard inside is shot the same way. First shot coming from the front door and the second shot standing over the body. He never had time to draw his weapon. Let's look at the bedrooms. Signs of a struggle. Sarah would not have gone without a fight. Cloth on the floor. Smells of ether. A bottle of ether on the nightstand. Makes sense. Had to get them out without noise. They surprised her. She struggles. They take her out with ether. Let's check Jamie's room. No signs of a struggle. Must have used ether while he was sleeping. The shooter probably went to get the car while the others got Sarah and Jamie. Check everything for prints, but you won't find any. Likely went out the back gate where it was dark. We know the timeline is between 03:00 and 05:00. They've got an 18 hour head start. Not going to be easy to track. Could be anywhere by now. Let's get to Pendleton and get some information. Call Pendleton and find out if any three-man teams are working in this area."

SIX

Camp Pendleton, California

"Sir, where are General Stevens and Director Turner working?"

"S.E.A.L Team operations headquarters."

"I need to get my team on standby, Sir. I want men I know and can trust for this, Sir."

"I already had that taken care of. I figured you would want them. Once we get the intel we need, you can read them in on this."

"Thank you, Sir."

"Attention! Commandant on deck!"

"As you were. General Stevens, what have you got for us?"

"Well Sir, we have three known teams fitting the bill working in the area for the highest bidder. Checked their financials and two of the three received large payments yesterday. One of those is laying low in the area. The other is not to be found anywhere. The third received a large payment today. Still trying to confirm the whereabouts of the team members."

"Find them. They're the ones that did this. They got payment after confirming the job was done. The other got paid to throw us off. Whoever did this is well connected and has the money to pull it off. Smells like the Medellin Cartel to me. Baker has to be involved."

"Director Turner, what have you found out about Baker?"

"He has property in DC and his home state of California. He has a home in Napa Valley and a hunting cabin in the mountains at Big Bear. He also is a partner in a winery and vineyard in Napa Valley. He and his family are currently in their DC home. There's no activity at his home in Napa Valley or his cabin at Big Bear."

"I know where they are. They're at the winery. He knew we would be watching his properties. But he thought nobody would think to look at a public winery with lots of coming and going. Assemble my team at our staging area. Nobody do anything until I say so."

Travis meets his team at the staging area and gets ready to brief them.

"Hello Marines. We have a situation. This isn't like anything we have faced before. We have walked down many roads and done many things together in the past. It was never personal before. This time it is. I love you guys and I know you love me. We have always had each other's backs. That being said, I totally understand if any or all of you decide this isn't for you this time. Someone has taken my wife and son."

"Holy shit!!!"

"Yeah, that's what I said. I'll do anything and everything in my power to get them back and I do mean anything. Legal or illegal, I'll do it. I know you guys have lives and families of your own, and I'm not going to ask you to do anything to jeopardize that. I know where they are and I'm putting together a plan. Four Marines lost their lives trying to protect them. The killers are professional and well-trained people. They don't think twice about taking lives. That's the mind set I'm going into this with. I'll harm, mame, kill or destroy anything and everything and anybody that stands in my way. I'll destroy the world if I have to. The real bitch is there is a high-ranking Senator involved in all of this. That's why I understand if any or all of you stand down on this. I'm going to inform the families of the four dead Marines. I want you to think about it and I'll talk to you when I get back. I love you guys."

Travis leaves the men to make their choices and talk among themselves. He makes his way to the airfield and boards a private CIA jet. His journey to fulfill the sad duty of informing the families whose sons gave their lives trying to protect his family begins.

SEVEN

"Mr. and Mrs. Standavol, my name is Sergeant Travis Bones. I'm sorry to inform you that your son has been killed in the defense of his country."

"Noooooo!!! What happened?"

"If I could come in, I would like to explain what happened."

"Yes of course, come in please."

"Thank you. First, I would like to thank you for your son's service. He was an exemplary Marine. He was killed while defending my home and my wife and son. I was deployed and we received word that someone was trying to get to my family. He was part of a four-man security team assigned to protect them. I wanted to be the one to personally inform you and the other families. Your son was a fine man and Marine. You will never know how grateful I am and how sorry I am."

"Are your wife and son ok?"

"No ma'am. They're currently missing."

"Oh my God!! Why are you here and not looking for them?"

"I wanted to be the one to inform you about your son because he gave his life for my family. I wanted to show you and your family the respect that his sacrifice demands."

"Thank you for that. But you need to go find your family."

"Thank you, Mr. and Mrs. Standavol."

"Mr. and Mrs. Flair, my name is Sergeant Bones, I'm sorry to inform you that your son has been killed in the defense of his country."

"Ooooohhhhhh my God noooo!!"

"If I could come in, I would like to explain what happened."

"We just talked to him two days ago. Come in, I have all kinds of questions."

"Yes ma'am."

"How did this happen?"

"He was part of a four-man security team assigned to protect my home and family until I got back from deployment. They surprised the team and all four were killed. I'm so sorry for your loss. He was a fine man and Marine. You will never know how sorry I am. I wanted to personally inform you about your son. I wanted to show you and your family the respect that his sacrifice demands."

"Thank you for that. I know this can't be easy for you. Is your family safe?"

"No ma'am. They're currently missing."

"Thank you for coming and showing your respect for our son. That means a lot to our family. Now go find your family Sergeant."

"Thank you, ma'am."

"Mr. and Mrs. Hernandez, my name is Sergeant Bones. I'm sorry to inform you that your son has been killed in defense of his country."

"Please tell me this is a horrible joke."

"I'm sorry to say that this is not a joke, ma'am."

"What the Hell happened?"

"He was part of a four-man security team dispatched to guard my home and family while I was deployed. We got word my family was in danger. All four of the team members were killed. You will never know how sorry I am. He was a fine man and Marine. I wanted to personally inform you of your son's death to show the respect for you and your family that his sacrifice demands."

"Thank you for that. Is your family safe?"

"No ma'am. They're currently missing."

"I'm sorry. Please go find your family!!"

"Thank you. I will."

"Mr. and Mrs. Penya, my name is Sergeant Bones. I'm sorry to inform you that your son has been killed in defense of his country."

"No, no, no, no, no!! This can't be happening. I'm not supposed to bury my son. He's supposed to bury me. How did this happen?"

"I was on deployment and we got word someone may try to get to my family. Your son was part of a four-man security team sent to guard my home and family. All four members were killed. I want to tell you how sorry I am for your loss. Your son was a fine man and Marine. I personally wanted to inform you and your family to show you the respect that his sacrifice demands."

"Thank you. How is your family?"

"They're missing."

"Oh my god!!! I'm so sorry."

"Thank you. If you don't mind, I'll go and try to find my family."

"Good luck Sergeant. I hope they're all right."

EIGHT

Camp Pendleton, California

"Alright gentlemen, I've done what I needed to do. There has still been no contact from anyone or demands given. There's only one reason for that to happen. They know I will not allow that to happen and they know I'll come after them to get my family back. They're counting on that to try to take me out. Gentlemen, I'll by the grace of God, give them that opportunity!!! I have given you time to think about this and talk to your families. I need to know if you're with me on this. What say you one and all?"

"We have talked to our families and we have talked as a team. We took an oath to become Marines. We don't take that oath lightly. We're all Uncle Sam's Misguided Children. We fight together, we die together. Semper Fidelis. So, say us all!!!"

"Semper Fidelis Marines!! Let's go wreak havoc and mayhem upon those against us!! Let's go unleash Marine Recon force upon the world!! Roll call. Spider."

"All in."

"Boomer."

    "All in."

    "Muskrat."

    "All in."

    "Falcon."

    "All in."

    "Squeaker."

    "All in."

    "Guardian."

    "All in."

    "Beaver."

    "All in."

    "Trojan."

    "All in."

    "Brutus."

    "All in."

    "Merlin."

    "All in."

    "Genius."

    "All in."

    "Tinker."

    "Gone, but never forgotten."

    "Digger."

    "Gone, but never forgotten."

    "Gadget."

    "Gone, but never forgotten."

    "Dragonslayer." "All in."

"Our objective, Marines, is a winery and vineyard in Napa Valley. Its 1,000 acres. Here are the aerial maps of the property. They chose this property, thinking we wouldn't notice traffic in and out of a public place, that being the rub here. We have innocents to look out for and to protect. Genius, you scout and provide intel. Falcon, you've got aerial intel. Guardian, Trojan and Merlin, you protect the innocents. Spider, Boomer and Muskrat, once we know which building, you have breach detail. Squeaker, monitor all locals and military. Beaver and Brutus, you have target detail. I'll be on overwatch. Wheels up in 20, gentlemen."

NINE

Napa Valley, California

"Ok gentlemen. The target is Oakville Winery. One thousand acres. Six hundred and thirty acres of vineyards and over 300 acres of preserve and family estate. It's been here since 1903. Let's try not to destroy it unless we have to. Belongs to the Pelissa family. We're coming in on the other side of the ridge from them. We'll split up on the ground and meet up at the top side of the property 500 yards out. That'll be the staging area. We'll gather intel and move out from there. We move at dark. Keep your head up and your asses down. Get ready to drop. First team, steps up. Green light. Five, four, three, two, one. Line clear. Second team, step up. Green light. Five, four, three, two, one. Clear. All right, going dark now. Another day in paradise. Thirty-degree uphill grade, 90 pounds of gear in late August in California. Hikers to the left of me."

"Form up on me. Squeaker, get coms up. Genius and Falcon, get me intel. Make it legit.

Genius, keep your head up and ass down. I got your back. Check public buildings first, then start with secondary structures. Save the house for last. Squeaker, I need any and all layouts for the buildings so we don't go in blind. Guardian, Trojan, Merlin and Boomer, corner watch. Squeaker, what's the traffic?"

"Green across the board, Skipper."

Travis recalls how each member of his team got their call signs.

Genius, aka Cpl. Leon Hatfield, can get into or around any security systems. He can get into anywhere or anything.

Falcon, aka Cpl. Lee Davis, is in charge of all aerial intel from satellites to calling in airstrikes and all things aerial in between.

Guardian, aka Cpl. Lewis Turner, is responsible for securing all locals and innocents involved in all operations.

Trojan, aka Cpl. William Smith, is responsible for any and all diversions needed to complete operations. He is very creative.

Merlin, aka Cpl. Terry Wilson, is our wizard in residence. He makes magic happen when we need it to happen. He can take a Volkswagen and make it appear to be a battleship.

Spider, aka Cpl. Thomas Massey, is our expert at climbing and rappelling. He can climb a glass wall and never leave a fingerprint.

Boomer, aka Cpl. Richard Jones, is the explosives expert. He can blow a hole the size of a dime or big enough to float a carrier through.

Muskrat, aka Cpl. David Thomas, is our resident water expert. He's a real-life aqua man.

Beaver, aka Cpl. Robert Stanfield, is our blockade man. He provides blocking anywhere it's needed.

Brutus, aka Cpl. Wilson Plumer, is the muscle in the group. He never goes down and can move anything from people to walls.

Squeaker, aka Cpl. Peter Hernandez, is in charge of communications. He can find anybody or anything that has a frequency.

Tinker - killed in action. He could take two screws and duct tape and build an atom bomb.

Digger - killed in action. He took care of all things subterranean and anything needing uncovering.

Gadget - killed in action. He took care of making anything needed to complete the mission.

I'm called Dragonslayer, aka Sgt. Travis Bones. I do sniper and overwatch detail. I take care of the guys and remove any threat to the mission. The team calls me Skipper and I run the team and operations.

"Squeaker, I need intel yesterday."

"Roger, Skipper. There are two men on the front door to the winery. There are five more around the equipment shed 15 feet to the left. Three vehicles not belonging to the winery are parked under the trees behind the equipment shed."

"Falcon, confirm."

"Roger, Skipper, confirmed."

"The two at the front door have earpieces and look to be armed. The five around the equipment shed have earpieces too. They're visibly armed. They're playing the shell game. Less is more. They have them in the winery. They want us to come to the shed. We assume they know I'm not alone."

"Genius, breach the fence and get me exact locations for all outside bodies. The five at the shed are hired to draw us to the equipment shed. The two at the door are the original team that did the grab. There will be one more of the original team somewhere. Most likely inside with the hostages. Guardian, Trojan, Merlin, protect the house and stop anyone coming in to the winery. Spider, Boomer, Muskrat, get ready to take out the two at the front door and wait for my command to breach. Beaver and Brutus, get ready to snatch and grab on my command. Squeaker, find their frequency and jam it on my command."

"Everyone go to com two now. Guardian, status."

"The five at the shed are as follows: one on each corner, one watching vehicles."

"Squeaker, you got that frequency yet?"

"Roger, Skipper."

"Jam it now. Guardian, take out the target at vehicles. Check vehicles for keys. Spider, status."

"In position, Skipper."

"Roger that. Hold for my command. Falcon, have support on standby."

"Roger, Skipper."

"Spider, Boomer, Muskrat, drop back and coordinate the strike with Genius at the shed. You have the green light to execute when ready."

"Roger that."

"Beaver, Brutus, standby for Spider, Boomer and Muskrat to execute."

"Roger that Skipper, holding."

"Support on standby, Skipper."

"Roger that. Genius, status."

"Targets down. Keyes secured. Three bugouts to position, Skipper."

"Roger that. Spider, status."

"In position, Skipper."

"Squeaker, how are we looking?"

"Green lights across the board, Skipper."

"Roger that. Everyone go to com three now. Genius, secure bodies in vehicles."

"Roger that."

"Boomer, hang back on the breach in case we find a surprise. Spider, green light to execute with a soft breach."

"Roger the soft breach, Skipper."

"Outside targets are down. Breaching the door now."

As the team enters the doorway, the target shouts:

"Stop!! Look down gentlemen. That mat is a pressure switch. It's wired to the explosives behind you on the wall. In addition, notice a thumb plunger in my hand. That's wired to the mat also. If you shoot me, you die. Notice I also have your family tied to that tank. The guns are pointed to them. I have another thumb plunger in my other hand. It's wired to the guns. Shoot me - they die. Here is what's going to happen. You're going to call your man in, and he will come unarmed. I'll kill him in front of his family, and then you can all go. Call him now."

"Skipper, we have a problem."

"What is that?"

"We're on a pressure mat wired to a thumb plunger the target's holding. Shoot him and we die. Good news is, Sarah and Jamie are here and alive. Bad news is, he has guns trained on them wired to another thumb plunger he's holding. Shoot him and they die. He wants you to come down unarmed. He said he's going to kill you in front of your family and then let us and them go."

"Bullshit. He'll kill me, then them, then you. Tell him I'm on my way. Unarmed. Boomer get eyes on the situation and get me a viable firing solution. I need it yesterday."

"Roger, Skipper."

"He's coming down unarmed."

"Falcon, get support hovering close by. That son of a bitch does not leave here alive!!"

"Roger that."

"Boomer, I need that solution now."

"I can get to the wires going to the mat, but the ones going to the guns I can't. Can't tell which plunger goes to which one."

"Ok, here's the plan. Genius, you come in the back door when I enter the front. Boomer, on my command you get the wires to the mat. The target will not let me get close because he knows I'll try to grab his hands. He can't shoot me because both his hands are busy. He either has someone else there or he has a plan I don't know about. I think he'll try to shoot Sarah and Jamie in front of me and then shoot me. He'll probably try to blow us all up after he shoots them. Genius, on my command take him out and I'll rush him and try to get to the plunger before he releases it. Shoot him at the base of the skull and shatter the spinal cord. That may keep him from releasing the plunger. It's very risky but I don't have any other options. Spider, you guys don't move off the mat until Boomer checks everything. Spider and Merlin, on my command, shoot the guns. Brutus and Beaver, take out anyone that might pop up. Everyone wait for my command. The command will be, 'Where is Senator Baker?' Execute on Baker. Tell him I'm coming in."

"Roger that Skipper."

"He's coming in."

"So, we finally get to meet face to face Sergeant. I expected you to be bigger."

"So, you're the low life son of a bitch that sold his country out for a few coins. Too bad you won't live long enough to spend it."

"On the contrary Sergeant. I'll spend mine and their shares. I'm assuming since I can't raise my men that you've dispatched them all?"

"Just like I'm going to do to you, you rat faced bastard."

"I really don't think you're in any position to make such an assumption."

"Where is Senator Baker?" Shots are heard.

"Sarah, are you and Jamie ok?"

"Yes, I think so!!"

"Gentlemen, clean it up and get ready to go." Sergeant Bones cuts his wife and son loose.

"I love you Sarah. I'm so sorry this happened."

"What in the Hell was this all about?"

"My last mission. We found a mole in the government and I couldn't get to you before they did. Come here and hug Daddy, Jamie. I love you so very much!! Do you know that?"

"Yes, Daddy."

"Don't you ever forget that, ok?"

"Ok, Daddy. I love you too."

"Falcon, cut support loose. Squeaker, break it down. Everyone meet at the equipment shed. We're going to base. Let's get you and Jamie to safety. We aren't finished yet. Squeaker, inform the Director and the General we are headed in and to have an ID team ready."

"Roger that, Skipper."

"Let's move out, everyone."

TEN

Camp Pendleton, California

Travis Bone's world seemed right at the moment. His family's safe, and his team is in one piece. God is good today. If he only knew what the next few days held in store for him, maybe he wouldn't be so complacent. Once at the base, Sarah and Jamie are debriefed and put in a car to go stay with friends in San Diego. Travis stays behind to find out who the men were that took them. He wants to find out how far up the chain this goes and what they can prove and not prove. He wants to trace the men and money to the source.

Sarah and Jamie say their goodbyes to Travis and head down the coastal highway to San Diego. If Travis sends them to see friends in San Diego at the base, nobody will be looking for them there and his friends will keep them safe until he can get there. Little does Travis know this will be the last time he sees his family alive.

"General Stevens Sir, have we found out the names of these guys yet?"

"Yes Sergeant, we have. The bodies belong to the three teams that received payment. All except one. He's not among the bodies. We are one body short of having three teams."

"Do we know who he is and where he is right now?"

"We know who he is, but we can't find him anywhere that he should be. His name is Don Williamson. He is ex-S.E.A.L. and a nasty piece of work. He was dishonorably discharged after he went rouge on his team, killing two and injuring three. He was part of S.E.A.L. Team Three. I believe you trained some with those boys, didn't you Travis?"

"Yes Sir, I did. Good bunch of soldier's, Sir. I always thought there was a little something off with Williamson. Something just didn't set right about him."

"He did this and disappeared before we could get him. We've been looking for him ever since. We never did come up with a reason until we heard he was running a three-man team on the black market. Nothing seems to be sacred to this man. He would kill his own mother if the price was right. I guess in his case, money talks."

"Squeaker, Boomer, Brutus, I need you to hit the road and find Sarah and Jamie. Make sure they're safe and bring them back here where we can watch them and keep them safe. Falcon, get a bird in the air and find them and keep overwatch until the boys get to them."

"Roger that, Skipper."

"You don't think he would go after them now, do you?"

"That's exactly what I think. He knew we would come in hard and fast to get them. Dammit!!! He's the safeguard. I should have caught that when we first saw how many men were on scene. This is my fault!!!"

"Stand at ease Sergeant. You can't think of everything all the time, soldier."

"Begging your pardon Sir, that's exactly what you trained me to do and what you expect each and every time we go out, Sir. That's why we are 300 and zero, Sir. All 300 missions we have run, we won because of just that. The one time it matters most, and I screw the pooch!!!! Dammit!!!! Excuse me Sir, but I need to take a minute to get back in the game."

Travis Bones walks out of the room. He finds the chapel and does something he hasn't done in a very long time. He falls to his knees and asks God to please keep his family safe until they can be brought securely back. Travis has not talked to God in a very long time. He thinks that with what he does for a living, God wouldn't listen or understand how he could break the commandments and still be saved.

"God, I know I have not been a good Christian. I know I have failed you in every way possible, but please God, I'm asking you to help keep my family safe until I can get them here and protect them. I promise to become a good Christian and raise my family in the church if you will only do this one thing for me. I know I'm not worthy of asking for this, but I AM asking for this. Please God, save my family. They should not have to suffer for my sins. I already have to live with what I've done. Don't punish them for my sins." Travis slowly rises and walks back toward destiny.

"What the Hell do we know about the money and where it came from?"

"We know the money came from the cartel, but I doubt we'll ever be able to prove it. We know that the only person that could have given your name up is Senator Baker, but what we don't know is how he got the info. We're still working to find out how."

"Director Turner, who besides yourself had access to the information?"

"No one that I know would have access. The file was kept in my private safe in my office. Oh my God, my secretary has the combination. He must have gotten to her. I don't know how or when, but you can damn well bet that I'm about to find out. Excuse me while I make a call and get the ball rolling."

"Falcon, do we have eyes on my wife and son yet?"

"Negative Skipper. Nothing yet. They should be there in about two minutes."

"Roger that, keep me up to date."

"Roger, Skipper."

"My secretary didn't come in to work today. I have a bolo out for her. We're checking her residence and all known acquaintances. We'll find her. We are also checking all routes out of the country and out of DC where she lives."

"When you find her, bring her here. I want to talk to her personally."

"As do I Sergeant Travis, as do I."

"General Stevens, may I have a word in private, Sir?"

"Gentlemen, give us the room please. What's on your mind Sergeant?"

"Sir, with all due respect, I'd like to have Director Turner's access to intel limited for the time being Sir, at least until we can rule him out as having a hand in this, Sir."

"I think that would be a good idea. I don't like thinking he would be involved, but Hell; I didn't expect Baker to be involved either!! I'll handle taking care of that. That way, he doesn't get mad at you and do something stupid. I just don't really trust those boys at Langley. They have screwed up too many times in the past for me to trust them."

"I totally agree Sir, but he might be a good asset later down the line if he's not involved. I don't want to screw the pooch at Langley unless we have to, Sir."

"Good point Sergeant."

"Skipper, the bird is on scene. It doesn't look good. There's been an accident. The car is over the side in a raven. It's on fire, Skipper."

"Where are Squeaker and the boys?"

"Arriving on scene now, Skipper. They're making their way down to the car now to check. Skipper, they said there are two bodies in the fire that they can see."

"NNNNNNNOOOOOOOOO!!!!!!!!

GOD NNNNNOOOOOOOOO!!!!"

Travis Bones drops to his knees and sobs uncontrollably. The boys come to his side, but even they can't console him. No one will ever be able to console him again. Travis Bones fills with rage for God, whom he feels let him down when he needed him most. At himself for missing the one thing that would have saved their lives. At Senator Baker, for starting this all-in motion. At Williamson for what he did to his family and most of all, rage at the cartel for funding this madness!!!!! He will never be the same man he was ten short minutes ago. His heart has died and, in its place, will grow something very cold and very, very evil. The face of the landscape and his very life itself will be changed forever. His very first thought is - kill them all and let God himself sort it out. Everyone must die

ELEVEN

Travis Bones awoke to what seemed like a dream. Then he slowly realized he had awakened in Hell instead. But Hell could not and would not be able to hold him in check. Hell was about to be unleashed upon the world and anyone involved in his family's death. Today he would find out what happened to his wife and son. Today he would make plans to bury them. Today his world officially ends, and his new life begins.

Travis called his family and Sarah's family to let them know what had happened. He could not bring himself to tell them the truth. He simply told them they were taking a trip to San Diego to visit friends when the car ran off the road and went down a ravine, bursting into flames. He nor they would be able to see them again. Because of the fire, he had to have the caskets sealed. He nor they would be able to kiss them goodbye.

Travis found out that they were forced off the road and down the ravine. Williamson had followed them down, shot each one in the head, and then set the car on fire. There will be a special place in Hell for him when he finds him. It will be slow and oh so painful before Travis lets him go to that place.

Travis had gone to the funeral home and made all the arrangements. Everything was ready for the funeral. Travis had talked to General Stevens and Stevens had told Travis that Travis wouldn't be able to be at the funeral. Travis remembered telling Stevens that he would be at the funeral and anyone trying to stop him would get hurt, starting with him. Stevens tried to order him not to go. Travis snapped and grabbed Stevens and beat the living Hell out of him. Travis knew why Stevens said what he said, but it didn't matter to him. Travis knew the General was trying to protect him. But another thing Travis knew was that no one was stopping him from being at the funeral. Travis told Stevens that Williamson wanted him to be at the funeral. That Williamson would be watching and laughing the whole time. Stevens asked him how he knew he wouldn't do anything. Travis explained that Williamson would want to enjoy the pain that he and the families would go through. He will come for Travis later. What he doesn't realize is that Travis will be hunting him, not the other way around.

Stevens told Travis that he understood and wouldn't do anything to him for hitting him. Travis said he could do whatever the Hell he wanted to because the world was about to change for them both. He could do it now or later. It didn't matter to Travis. Stevens told Travis that if he tried to follow up on this, he would be discharged from the corps with a general discharge and might face federal charges. It was the best he could do for Travis. Travis became enraged and told Stevens to go ahead and do what he had to do because he was not going to sweep this under the rug and act like his family was still here and that nothing had happened. Anyone and everyone involved in any way in this deal would be held accountable to him personally. Travis told him to consider this his resignation effective immediately.

"Excuse me Sir, I have a funeral to attend."

TWELVE

Houston, Texas

Travis Bones had arrived in Houston, Texas early on the morning of September 21st and checked into the hotel. He was dressed and ready for the car from the funeral home to pick him up. He had decided to be the only one speaking at the funeral. No preacher or priest or any man of God would be in attendance. He had too much rage in his body to allow that to happen today.

The car arrived and Travis slowly got in the back seat. Travis didn't like funerals as a general thing, but today seemed like each minute lasted an hour. He knew he was going to say goodbye to the two people in this world that meant everything to him and defined him as a person. That person had died when they did. Right now, he had to find some way to control the rage boiling inside of him and he had no idea how he was going to make that happen.

When the car arrived at the chapel, all Travis could feel was sorrow and pain. Pain for himself, his family and Sarah's family. He got out and was greeted by his mom and dad. He looked around and there were his brother and sisters. They hugged and cried and held each other. Then he saw Sarah's mom and dad and brother. They looked like they were yet to believe this was really happening. Travis knew the feeling well. He greeted them and hugged them and tried to tell them how sorry he was. As they entered the chapel a strange calm came over him and he did not understand, but he now had control over his rage. He would not, could not let the families see this. He had no idea what he would say until this moment. He knew it was Sarah doing this to him. She could always calm him, and he knew she was doing this even from the grave. His heart lightened for a moment and he proceeded to the altar.

"I would like to thank everyone for coming today. We are here to celebrate the lives of Sarah Hines Bones and James Henry Bones - the lights in my life. I remember the first time I ever saw Sarah. I was dating her roommate, Sue. I went over to pick up Sue and Sarah answered the door. It was like I had been hit in the chest. The long brown hair and the dazzling blue eyes - she captured my heart from the first moment I saw her. I just knew I had to spend time getting to know her. Sue was not there so I asked her if she wanted to get something to eat. She said sure, and the rest is history. I asked her to marry me six weeks later and she said yes. I thought I was the happiest man in the world. I became happier three months later when she told me that she was pregnant. I had never known happiness like that in my life. Our son was born healthy and happy and we were on cloud nine. I didn't think life could be any better. As time went on, we only loved each other more deeply.

Sarah and Jamie were the light in my day and the very air that I breathed. I have to do a lot of ugly things in my line of work, but no matter how dark or ugly things got, I always had that light at the end of the tunnel - my loving wife and son. They saved me from all the bad things in this world. Now I don't have that anymore and my world has become dark and empty. I don't know if I'll ever be able to find that light and love again. I can only carry their love and memories in my heart and use their love to lift me up. I only hope that the rest of you can do the same.

That's what Sarah and Jamie are all about. They don't want us to grieve at the loss of them but carry their love in our hearts and lives and be joyous to have known them. They may be gone from this mortal earth, but they will live forever in our hearts and memories. They were always there for each and every one of us and I know that we'll be there for them now. Let us now lay them to rest and say our goodbyes and celebrate their lives. I want to thank my brothers in arms for being here and being the pallbearers and helping me lay my family to rest today. Sarah loved each and every one of you. I look forward to the day I'll be reunited with them both. Thank everyone again for coming today and may God bless each of you."

Travis watched as if in a dream as the caskets were loaded and unloaded and lowered in the ground. He wasn't sure he would be able to walk to get back to the car. Nothing seemed to be working in his body right now. He was hoping it was all some sick dream and he would wake up and find everything fine, but he knew that would not happen. He barely could focus as people streamed past to pay their respects.

He was grateful that they came and cared, but he just wanted to be alone, to give in to his rage and grief. He wanted to hurt something and get started on what he knew could not bring his family back but would settle the score and give him some sense of justice and peace of mind. He didn't like thinking like this, but the light was gone, and only darkness stood before him. He knew the darkness and he welcomed it with open arms. He wanted now to be consumed by it to ease the pain. He didn't know if he would ever see the light again and with this realization, he smiled. He had become comfortable with the dark. It was warm and wrapped around him like a blanket and he was home.

THIRTEEN

Oceanside, California

Travis decided he needed to take some time to pack up his home and put together his plan. He called Stevens and told him he was taking 30 days to get his things in order. Travis went about packing up his life and home and putting it in storage. Once he was finished, he felt drained and empty. His whole world was packed in a ten by twenty storage bin. He needed to reenergize himself and get his plans together. Travis decided he would take a trip but needed to figure out where. Suddenly, he smiled. He had the perfect place. Since Baker wasn't using his cabin at Big Bear, he might as well. Maybe he could learn more about him while he was there.

Travis packed a bag and headed out the door. It would take about three hours to get to Big Bear. He would wait until dark to go up to the cabin and make sure that no one was watching it or staying there. He stopped at Thelma's restaurant for dinner. He had prime rib, baked potato, salad and iced tea. For dessert he had a piece of homemade lemon pie. He felt full and content. He would wonder around town like a tourist until he was ready to go to the cabin.

Travis got back to his car and headed up West Big Bear Boulevard to Greenway Drive. From there he would go to 40147 North Shore Drive. The cabin was on the lake. Travis pulled down the drive and pulled into the garage. He got out and shut the garage door, then went about 100 yards in the woods to watch for company. He waited till nine thirty. Seeing no movement or signs of anything out of the ordinary, he headed to the house. He easily found a key hidden under a plant on the back deck. He checked and found the wires for the alarm system and circumvented the alarm. He then entered the house of his enemy. He began putting together his plan to bring the responsible persons to pay for their involvement in this tragedy. He went about learning the layout of the cabin to set up a defense if anyone came around. First things first. Since he was working in the dark, he put the red lens in his flashlight. That way there's no bright light for the neighbors to see and he keeps his night vision intact in case someone decides to visit.

"Let's start finding out about his family. Look for pictures. Here we go, looks like he has a daughter and a son. The daughter looks to be mid to late 20's, son looks to be early 20's. Graduation pictures from Ivy League schools. Wife looks like she may be a few years younger than the Senator. Let's find the Senator's office and see what we can come up with. Here we go. Ok, let's see what he has in his drawers. Locked. What are we trying to hide, Senator?

Nothing a knife blade can't fix. Looks like a Senator would buy better quality locks. Oh well, makes it easier for me. Ok, standard nongovernmental bull shit, bills, correspondence, press clippings, standard office supplies. This drawer seems just a little bit shallower than the rest. Ah hah! A false bottom. Let's see what we have here. Pictures of me and my family, my house, our vehicles, three deposit slips, each for $1,000,000. Well, this definitely puts the Senator involved. It looks like he orchestrated everything from here, which means he was here possibly as late as a few days ago. Intel said he was in DC with his family. We need to look into the son and daughter. Maybe one of them is trying to protect Daddy. That paints a horse of a different color."

Travis decided he needed to make a trip to Langley and have a talk with Director Turner. Travis finished searching the house without finding anything new. He tossed his bag in the car and backed out with no lights on. He had a long drive ahead and a lot of time to think.

FOURTEEN

Cross Country Road Trip

Travis stopped in town at a phone booth, pulled a card out of his pocket, and dialed the number.

"We need to talk. Not on the phone. I'll be there in three days. We'll meet in the Memorial Garden at two o'clock."

Travis hung up and got in the car. He decided to take 18 North out of town to 247 at Lucerne Valley. He would take 15 at Barstow, and then hit 70 in Utah. He would follow 70 to Fredrick, Maryland, then 495 to Georgetown Pike in Mclean, Virginia and on to 1000 Colonial Farm Road. He had three days and 2600 miles to try to figure things out. Where was he to start and where would it lead? He hoped he would have an answer or at least some idea of how the information he found tonight played into all of this. He knew in his heart that the deposits were to the groups that they knew, but he needed to prove it. Follow the money and he could take it back to the cartel. With no deposit slip going to any of Baker's accounts, Travis figured that the cartel delivered cash to Baker or whomever was coordinating this whole thing for them.

This whole thing started when the government wanted to put an operation into effect to try to get intel on the cartel and try to take out operations to slow them down and cost them money. They couldn't put the whole team in without making too big of a footprint, so Travis had agreed to go in alone and the team would be support and intel for him. Travis had cost them millions in money and time to rebuild operations he took out. He had cost them family and the cartel took that personally. Now Travis was taking it personally also. Someone was going to pay and pay with family!!!

Their northern operations were in shambles and it would take a long time for them to get everything operating again. This worked to Travis's advantage. He knew where they would be and who would be there. Travis estimated that he had eliminated at least 80 to 100 of the cartel's men during the operation. Travis knew his career was in the crapper now and before he was through it would not be salvageable.

Travis was a highly decorated Marine. He had received the Purple Heart, two Bronze Stars, one with Oak Leaf Clusters, the Silver Star, Presidential Unit Citation, Defense Superior Service with Bronze Cluster, Navy and Marine Corps Medal, Meritorious Service Medal, Navy Marine Corps Commendation, Marine Corps Good Conduct and the Marine Corps Expeditionary Medal. He had met President Carpenter and had dinner at the White House.

"Now look at my sad state of affairs."

It was 23:45. Travis decided he would drive through the night and sleep during the day. His mind was running a 1000 miles an hour with the new information he'd found. This is what he was trained to do. Find intel and process it and come up with an action plan. This one is going to be tricky. He no longer had his back-up and support so he would have to improvise, adapt and conquer. That's just what Marines do. Travis settled in for the long drive and started thinking about Williamson and where he might be and how he could get to him. Travis had been going over everything he had read and knew about Williamson when he realized that the sun was coming up.

Suddenly, Travis pulled over to the side of the road and jumped out of the car. It hit him like a ton of bricks. He knew where Williamson was and how he could get to him. This was the way Travis wanted to start the day. He suddenly realized how tired he was and decided to stop and get some sleep. Travis got back in the car, found an open restaurant, and had breakfast. He asked the waitress where a good motel was, paid the bill, and headed there to sleep.

FIFTEEN

Coming into McLean, Virginia

CIA Headquarters

Travis woke up and looked at the clock. It was 17:30. Travis got cleaned up and headed out to get something to eat. As he was heading out, he stopped and looked at the reflection in the mirror. He was in game mode and this made him smile. He had already decided how he would handle Williamson and he was going to make it very slow and so very painful before he put out his lights for good.

"Ok, I have to find out more about Baker's kids before I can figure out who was at the lake cabin at Big Bear. I'm leaning toward the son, but the daughter may be a daddy's girl. First, I have my meeting, and then get an intel update about the kids."

Travis ran all the possible scenarios in his head for the next two nights while driving. He pulled into Mclean, Virginia at 02:30 of the third day. He found a motel and checked in.

Travis awakes to the sounds of the phone ringing. He answers and it's his wake-up call. He looks at the clock and its 12:00. His meeting is in two hours. Travis gets cleaned up and heads out to get something to eat. He's hoping things will go swiftly after the meeting.

At 13:55, Travis was sitting on the bench in the northeast corner of the Memorial Garden at 1000 Colonial Farm Road in Mclean, Virginia. At 14:02 he was joined by Director Turner of the CIA.

"Thank you for seeing me, Director."

"My pleasure, Sergeant Bones. How are you holding up?"

"Actually, I'm doing fine, thank you for asking. I have some very interesting things to show you, Sir."

Travis hands him a package with documents from the senator's home office at Big Bear Lake.

"Where did these items come from?"

"Senator Baker's desk at Big Bear Lake. One of the drawers had a false bottom. Sir, have they found your secretary yet?"

"Not yet, but we're still searching."

"I hate to say it, but I don't believe they'll find her alive."

"What makes you say that, Travis?"

"Williamson, Sir. Whenever he's involved, bodies turn up."

"You have a very valid point. So, what are the items you found?"

Travis waits for Turner to look over and digest what he's just seen.

"So, Baker was directly involved in all this?"

"He was definitely involved, but to what degree I'm not sure yet."

"What do you mean?"

"The intel said he and his family were in DC when the deposits were done. So that means that someone in his family is either trying to protect him or was sent to do his dirty work. I need to get some intel on his kids."

"Travis, I heard what happened at Pendleton and I want to tell you I'm sorry. It's a shame that they would put you out after everything you gave them. I want you to know I admire and respect what you've done for this country and the professional restraint you've shown through all of this. I would love to have you work for me anytime, anyplace."

"I'm glad you feel that way, Sir. If you would allow me, I'd like to make you a proposal."

"I'm all ears, Travis."

"Thank you, Sir. First, I know that you have President Carpenter's ear. I'm ok with a general discharge as long as I'm allowed to play this out. I want no charges brought against me for anything that happens in the conclusion of all this. Second, I'm allowed to play this out with the full resources of the CIA to whatever the outcome may be. If I can bring them in to face true justice, I'll be happy with that. If not, justice will be dealt my way. Third, I want my team hired to work with me. Nothing personal Sir, but I don't know your people. I can trust my life to these guys. To be effective in this and for you Sir, that's what we need, both you and I. Fourth,

Williamson will receive my brand of justice, not the courts. I'll deal personally with him my way. It will not be pretty, that I guarantee. Fifth, my team and I become your go to team for black ops."

"Personally Travis, I have no problem with anything you've proposed. Let's get you inside and I'll introduce you to agent Walbach. You and Walbach can get started on gathering intel and I'll make a phone call. Are your boys on board with this whole thing?"

"I don't know yet, Sir. I'll call when we get inside and let you know."

"Shall we go inside?"

"You can use this phone. It's a secure line. I'll be outside when you get done." Travis dials the number for the ops room at Pendleton and Boomer answers. "Boomer, this is Bones. Are all the guys there?"

"Yeah Skipper, we're all here. What's up?"

"How would you guys like to work with me at the CIA?"

"You're serious, Skipper?"

"As a heart attack."

"Not yes, but Hell yes!!"

"Awesome, gear up and expect your travel papers within the hour. You're no longer Marines; you're now CIA black ops. See you soon. Guys, thank you."

"Roger that, Skipper."

"We're good to go Sir. The boys are gearing up and waiting for travel orders."

"Outstanding! I'll go make my call and get the paperwork going. If all goes well, they'll be here by 19:30. Agent Bones, this is Agent Walbach, Agent Walbach, this is Agent Bones. You're to assist him in any way he needs, and clearance is not a problem. I'll join you gentlemen shortly."

"Thank you, Sir."

"Agent Walbach, I need to find out everything I can about Senator Baker's family. His wife, daughter and son. Who lives at the DC residence and who doesn't - where they live and what they've been doing for the last month. I'm looking for any red flags - anything that's not their normal routine."

"Agent Bones, here are your credentials and weapon, and the President is on board with everything you've proposed. The travel orders have been sent and the boys should be getting on a plane right about now. You have the same security clearance as I do so you won't have any problems getting what you need. Once your men are here, get me a list of gear that you need, and I'll make it happen within two hours. I have three alias ID's for you with history you need to learn. I'll have the same for each member of your team when they arrive. In the package you just received, is an emergency alias and $100,000 cash. If this ID is activated, it will mean you've been compromised and we'll implement the evac plan in your package. Is all this clear, Travis?"

"Perfectly, Sir. The info will be learned and destroyed by the time the men arrive, Sir."

"Very good, Travis. Glad to see you've not forgotten your training."

Travis spends the next four hours learning his new alias and destroying the evidence. He also spends that time putting together a list of items he and the team will need to get started as a unit for this particular mission. Travis was soon to learn that the government has things the military can only dream of.

"Agent Bones, the Director wanted me to let you know that your team has just arrived and for me to take you to them."

"Thank you, Walbach. Let's go greet the boys."

Travis was led down a series of corridors and into an elevator. They dropped for a good 90 seconds before the elevator came to a stop. He was then led down a hallway and into a room where the team was waiting with Director Turner.

"Ok Travis, the men are here. We need to get them up to speed and on board with the plans you and I have made. This gentlemen, is your new ops center. Your ID's will get you into the rooms. Only myself and the team members will have access and knowledge of these rooms. Gentlemen, you're six stories under the CIA headquarters building. These rooms are fully self-contained and have separate backup systems from the rest of the facility. This is home when you're running missions and non-existent when you're not. Travis, I'll leave it up to you to explain things to the team."

"Yes, Sir."

"I'll leave you to it, men."

"It's good to see you guys again. Gentlemen, on the table in front of you is a package with your name on it. Stand in front of your package. In these packages are your ID's, as well as three other identities with histories. You'll need to know these and destroy them as soon as you learn them. They consist of driver's license, credit cards and passports. You will also find a separate and fourth ID. This ID is to be your emergency ID. Each of you has $100,000 in cash. We'll each deposit this in a Swiss safety deposit box along with your alias ID's. If you're in trouble or cover is blown, you get to the safety deposit box and activate your emergency ID and start your extraction plan. This will alert them at Langley, and they'll come for you according to plan. In the next four hours, you will learn your ID's and histories and make a list of what you'll need individually. This room is the Ops Center. The room to your left is the Com Center. The room to your right is the computer room. The rooms behind you are living quarters and bathrooms. This is home when we're on missions. Let's get started, men."

Travis gets on the phone with Walbach and has him send all the info on Baker's family to their new computer system. Travis spends the next four hours going through all the data.

Travis learned that Baker's son is 23 and lives at home. He was accounted for the time period that the deposits were made. The daughter is 27 and married to a federal prosecutor named Clarence Sears, who works for the District of Columbia. They live in the Georgetown area and his time is accounted for the time of the deposits. Baker's daughter, however, was at home and her whereabouts were unknown for the time frame of the deposits. Winner, winner, chicken dinner!!! Looks like Travis might be right about her being a daddy's girl. Travis needs to have the signatures on the deposit slips compared to her handwriting to be sure. Travis has Walbach compare the writings and signature and gets confirmation of what he suspected. Her name is Teresa Sears and she's the first link in the chain. Travis needs to confirm her location and plan a snatch and grab for her and her husband. Travis doesn't know if her husband is involved or not, but he needs to find out. Time to get with the boys and plan operation "Fly Trap".

SIXTEEN

Washington, DC

"Ok gentlemen, this will be operation Fly Trap. The objective is to snatch Clarence and Teresa Sears. No faces and no names. He's a Federal Prosecutor with the District of Columbia, and I don't know if he's involved in the actual events or if he's being played. In any event, we know she's involved, and we need to assess how much and how deeply she has knowledge. Daddy may have played her, or she may be as deeply involved as he is."

"They'll be dining at the Old Ebbitt Grill around 19:30 tonight. We'll wait till they head for their car and take them and the car then. We'll take them to The Barn and interrogate them there, separately. I don't want them together. The Barn is a CIA farm just outside of DC we can access when we need it. I want him questioned first and then I'll come in and talk to him. Is everyone clear on this?"

"Roger that, Skipper."

"Does everyone have their equipment list ready for the Director?"

"Here you go, Skipper."

"Awesome. Now I'll present our list to the Director and see how fast we can get the items. Get some rest till I get back, gentlemen. It may be a long few days. Squeaker, get these boys hooked with home. It might be awhile before they have a chance to again."

"Roger, Skipper."

"Director Turner, I have the equipment list that we need. How quickly do you think we can get these items, Sir?"

"Let's see, ok, ok, it looks like we should have all of these items on site. You should have them within the hour."

"Sir, for plausible deniability, I'm not going to brief you on the mission that we'll be undertaking tonight. I don't think you would want to know anyway. We'll probably be unavailable for a few days."

"I understand and appreciate your candor, Travis. Carry on."

"Alright men, we should have the equipment shortly. When we get it, I want ready packs made up and staged. I want gear double and triple checked and ready to go at a moment's notice. Are we clear on that?"

"Roger that, Skipper."

"I hope everyone got hooked up with home. Let's get rested up and ready for the next few days."

"Rise and shine gentlemen. We are two hours away from go time. It's time to gear up and stand ready. Genius, you wait at The Barn. Falcon and

Squeaker, you make sure we're clear on the ground and the air. Guardian, clear all locals from the area. Trojan, be ready if we need you. Merlin, Spider and Boomer, you're at The Barn. Brutus and Beaver are with me on snatch detail. Brutus takes the husband and Beaver will take the wife. I'll be overwatch in case we have a problem. Everyone clear?"

"Clear, Skipper."

"Mount up and let's roll!!!"

"Com check."

"Falcon and Squeaker"

"Clear."

"Guardian and Trojan."

"Clear."

"Brutus and Beaver."

"Clear."

"Overwatch is clear. On my command, gentlemen."

"Standby. Here they come. Caps on."

"GO!! GO!! GO!! Van is ready."

"Targets acquired. Coming Home."

"Trojan, Take the car. Let's roll."

"Gentlemen, get The Barn ready."

William E. Boone

SEVENTEEN

The Barn

"Clarence Sears, Federal Prosecutor for the District of Columbia, married to Teresa Sears, no children. We have some questions for you, and it would be best for you to answer truthfully and quickly. The longer it takes to get the answers, the rougher it'll be for you and your wife."

"Where's my wife?"

"She's safe for now. That's all you need to know."

"What's this all about?"

"We ask the questions genius; you give the answers. Or do we need to drive the point home?"

"Ok!! OK!!"

"You will notice that you're in a soundproof room with no windows and only one door. You'll also notice that you're strapped to a chair. Take a good look at the chair and you'll notice it has wires running to it. These wires are connected to 110 volts of power. Every time I deem that you give me a wrong answer, you'll receive a shock. It will start with a two second dose and go up two seconds every time you give me a wrong answer. Do you understand what's at risk here?"

"Yes, Sir I do, but you can't be serious about this. This is illegal!! I'm a Federal Prosecutor. Do you know how much trouble you're already in? If you let us go now, I'll make sure nothing happens and we'll forget this whole ordeal."

"Shut up. Let me make myself clear here. You have no rights as of this moment. I can and will do whatever it takes to get the answers I want. You have no idea where you are, or who I am. I can and will hold you for as long as I want to and do whatever I want to you. You're part of a group accused of crimes against your country, asshole, and if you keep talking, I'll flip the switch and walk away until you start smoking from the voltage!!!!"

"Where was your wife for the last couple of weeks?"

"She was at home."

"Wrong answer. Light him up." Sounds of electricity.

"Wait, she went on a trip to Oakville Winery in Napa a couple of weeks ago. Her father's a partner in the winery. What's this about?"

"Do I need to smack you to remember who asks and who answers the questions?"

"No."

"Ok. What did she go to the winery for?"

"Her dad asked her to go check on something to do with the winery. Said he couldn't get away right now."

"Does he have her do that often?"

"No. This was the first time, come to think about it."

"Did you know anything about your father-in-law having a meeting with the drug cartels in Columbia?"

"What the Hell are you talking about?"

"Was he out of the country a few weeks ago?"

"Yeah, something about a good will visit."

"His good will visit got a Marine's family killed and his life is in danger because he identified this Marine to them."

"I don't believe you."

"Then let me introduce you to the Marine in question and see if he can convince you, asshole."

"Did you know that while your wife was at the winery, she was really at his place in Big Bear making deposits for her father to pay for the hit teams?"

"What the Hell are you telling me?"

"I'm telling you your wife is directly responsible for the deaths of at least five people and possibly more to come because of her actions for her father."

"I knew they were a secretive family, but I never imagined anything like this. What proof do you have to confirm this?"

"Your father-in-law was confirmed and identified by Marines on the ground having meetings with cartel members. Your wife's handwriting has been confirmed to be the handwriting on the deposit slips making the deposits for the kill teams that killed the Marine's family and tried to kill him and his team. Shall I continue or is that enough to know that you and your wife are screwed?"

"Wait, I had nothing to do with any of this."

"If we find that to be true, you'll be set free. Your wife on the other hand will face justice. It's her choice as to what kind of justice she faces."

"Are you really going to let this asshole go, Skipper? You don't really believe him, do you?"

"Put him in isolation and let him think about what his wife and her family have done to him. To answer your questions, I think he was played by them and Hell no, he's not going free. Her answers will decide how and when they have their accident."

The look of utter fear on Clarence's face causes Travis to smile.

"Just giving him false hope is all I'm doing."

EIGHTTEEN

"Teresa Sears - married to Clarence Sears. No children. Daughter of Senator William Baker. I have some questions for you and depending on your attitude and answers, I can make this easy or as hard as it needs to be. Believe me when I say you want the easy way."

"What in the Hell is this about?"

"Your father being a treasonous bastard and selling his soul to the devil himself. My wife and son dying for something they knew nothing about. You following in your father's footsteps and selling your soul to the devil like he did. That's what this is about. You think the devil is bad, he runs and hides when he sees me coming. I'll do any and everything I need to do to get the answers. You just disappeared and whether you ever show back up depends on those answers. Are we clear now about why you're here?"

"I know nothing about what my father does in the Senate."

"This has nothing to do with him and the Senate. This is about him being in bed with the drug cartels and you helping him."

"I don't know what you're talking about."

"Wrong answer!!!!"

"Did you ever go deer hunting with your father?"

"Yes, why?"

"Did he teach you how to skin a deer?"

"Yes. Why are you asking me about this?"

"Can you imagine how painful that would be if you did that to a living human being? I can. I've seen it done in Columbia. Done to villagers by the cartel. Sometimes it would take days before they died. Do you get my drift?"

"Ooooohhhhhh my God!!!! You're talking about doing that to me!!! You would never get away with this. You sick bastard!!!"

"You and your father are the sick bastards. You had my family killed so you could line your pockets with money. No thought as to how it would affect anyone else but yourselves!!! No, I'm not the sick one here, but I'll enjoy it though. Depending on your answers as to how much skin you lose. Shall we begin to play the game?"

"Someone will hear me screaming and come to help!!!"

"You can and will scream as long and as loud as you want to, no one will hear you. We are 60 feet underground and the room is soundproof. Hell, no one in the next room will hear you, much less anyone outside. Your ass is mine and I'll get my answers. It's just a matter of how long it takes. I have everything I need to keep you alive until I get what I want."

"You're quite mad, aren't you? You've simply lost your mind, haven't you?"

"Oh no, my dear!! I have never been more laser focused. I'm going to bring you and your family's world down around your ears and there's not a damn thing you can do to warn them. It's time to start the questions. If I were you, I would think long and hard before I answered."

"How long have you known about your father's involvement with the cartels?"

"I don't know what you're talking about."

"Let's start with the soles of your feet, shall we?"

"OOOOHHHHHHH my God, noooooo!!!!!!"

Travis lifts her foot up and straps it to the board he has positioned in front of the chair. He starts at the ball of her foot just behind the toes and starts slicing and peeling the skin back until he reaches the heel. He clips the skin off and drops it in a bowl on the table. The entire foot is raw flesh and exposed nerves. Travis doesn't enjoy what he does, but it's a necessary evil he must do to get the answers he needs.

"The right foot is done. That has to hurt like a bitch, huh? Now, how long have you known about your father's involvement with the cartels?"

"I swear to God I don't know what you're talking about!!!"

"You need to talk to someone you know instead of God, whom you have no relationship at all."

"OOOOOOHHHH my God, nooooooo!!!!!!"

"You know, nerves are a very sensitive thing in general, but when they're raw, they can be extremely painful. I have some needles here that would be extremely painful if I were to stick them in the raw nerves. I think it would be so painful that you would pass out from it. What do you think?"

"PLEASE STOP!!!!! I can't take anymore. I'll tell you whatever you want to hear."

"Left foot is done. I don't want you to tell me what I want to hear. I want you to tell me the truth. One way or another you will tell me the truth or die protecting your daddy and his lies. Shall I start with the needles or are you going to tell me the truth?"

"What do you want to know?"

"That's a smart move. We shall see if that's the truth or not. Why did your father send you to the cabin in Big Bear?"

"He needed me to make some deposits for the winery. Said they needed the money for the harvest this year."

"And you really believed that? Did you not notice that the winery name was not on any of the deposit slips?"

"He said that it was going to individuals who were supplying labor for the harvest. I asked him about the names. That's what he told me. It seemed funny to me, but he insisted that it was for labor costs. I asked him how they could make a profit spending so much on labor and he assured me that that was normal; he just couldn't get away to make it himself. Something about a bill having to be voted on or something to that nature. I swear that's the truth!!"

"Do you expect me to stand here and swallow that load of horseshit???? You want me to believe that your father duped you into doing his dirty deeds by telling you the winery needed the money for the harvest? Do I look stupid or are you willing to die with that lie?"

"I didn't believe it either, so I did some digging on my own while I was there and found out that the winery had never heard of these people. I have a file with what I found in it."

"Where's this file? Did you confront your father about what you found out?"

"Yes, I did. He said the money was being given to some people in Columbia for information about the cartel and their operations so that we could stop the flow of drugs coming into the United States. He said Congress had funded the money to contacts he had made while he was in Columbia when he went down. That was why he went down - to confirm their information."

"He went down to take his pay off from the cartel for allowing drugs by the boat load to enter these United States. I know. I was there. I shot and blew up his contact. Does the last name Escobar ring a bell? That's the name he's in bed with. He gave them my picture and my family's information, and they came after them like the animals they are. They paid those names you sent money to shoot my wife and son and then burned their bodies in a car fire. Your father will pay for what he's done, but in my court, not the legal system's court. You and your husband will pay along with him. You're just as dirty as he is for helping him and believing his lies. Now where's this file you say you have?"

"It's in a safe at home. I, I can get it for you. You can go with me. I promise I won't contact anyone."

"You're not going anywhere. You'll give me the location and combination and my people will get the file."

"The neighbors will see your people and call the police."

"The neighbors will never see my people. We took you and your husband in public and no one saw a thing. It's what we do. No one will ever know we were there. Now give me the location and combination or I'll start moving up the leg."

"The safe is behind a painting in the library. The combination is 34-27-16-48. Could I please have something for the pain?"

"Guy's get in here. Get the medics to patch her up. Genius, Falcon and Brutus, go to her house and retrieve the file and get it back here. There may be more in it than she's telling us. Check the rest of the house while you're there. When the medics are done, put her back in isolation, then we all meet back at Langley Op's Center to see what we find."

NINETEEN

Langley Op's Center

"Ok men, what did we find?"

"We hit the jackpot, Skipper. She had files on all kinds of shady dealings her father's responsible for having done inside and outside of the government. This guy's a real piece of work. Your family's apparently not the first people he has taken care of and guess who his go to guy is? Apparently, he's the one that turned Williamson in the first place. He created Williamson to be his own personal hit team whenever he needed them. Looks like for the past several years, he's personally saying who wins and loses in the election all the way from local to national level. From what we've gathered, half of Capitol Hill is on his payroll. There are a lot of big names that owe him favors and some have already been called upon to pay up."

"This just proves that she knows what's going on and is up to her neck in everything. Either that or she's gathered enough intel to black mail or keep her father in check and off her back. Sounds like brother may be out in the cold if anything happens to daddy. Is the son or daughter mentioned in any of these files? We need to rule out the son, because if he's mixed up in all this, we need to deal with him also. Genius, see who the beneficiary is on her father's insurance and will, and see if the son's included in any of them."

"Roger that, Skipper. On it."

"Squeaker, find out what the son has been up to. I want to know it all, including if he stumped his toe for the last month."

"Roger, Skipper."

"Guardian, shadow the son in case we need to yank him. Keep Trojan in the loop so we can be prepared at a moment's notice."

"Roger, Skipper."

"The rest of us will finish going through the files and make our list of who we need to watch, speak to or yank if need be. This is going to be a long night. Grab some chow and get started, gentlemen. And I use that term loosely. Ha ha!!!"

TWENTY

The Barn

"Mrs. Sears, would you like to tell me about the secret room in your house willingly, or shall I continue with what I started?"

"What? How did you find out about it?"

"My men are very thorough and very professional. They don't miss much. They know what to look for. Now, do you want to tell me all about it or shall we continue. I personally don't think you can take too much more."

"Ok. I'll tell you. My father is a very powerful man. He holds a lot of power over his colleagues. I wanted to know how he held so much power, so I started looking into what he did and how he did it. He's consumed with power and all it entails. Hell, he would sell his own mother out if it benefited him and he got more power. I wanted to protect myself and my brother and mother, so I started collecting as much information as possible so that if he ever tried to screw us over, I would have power over him. I came to realize that a man like that would just have you killed and then destroy the evidence. That's why I built the secret room, so he couldn't find the evidence. I guess now, that was stupid on my part. If you could find it, I guess his people could too."

"Why gather the information on the others?"

"I wanted to know that if things ever went sour for my father, maybe I could use that information to help him."

"So, the good daughter till the very end, huh?"

"I realize now that was stupid on my part. I mean, he would have the same information as I did to use against them. Hell, probably a whole lot more than what I have for that matter. I just wanted to protect my family."

"Well, I thank you for doing the heavy lifting for me. I'll use that information to destroy your father and his circle of cohorts. He'll be publicly humiliated and run out of office along with his cronies. Then I'll make it look like he committed suicide because of it. Or, I may decide to kill him first and then humiliate him after his death. Either way, he dies. I just haven't decided how or when yet. But thanks to you, we'll be able to clean up the government somewhat, thanks to your information."

"What are you going to do to me and my husband? I have answered your questions. Can't you let us go with the promise not to tell anyone about any of this? Put us in witness protection or something?"

"I'm afraid that won't be possible. You see, your father had my family killed, so I'll have to do the same in return. I want him to go through what I had to. I'll spare your mother if I find that she's not involved. I understand your father's estate is worth between 40 to 50 million dollars, I think your mother would be ok living on that. Your brain-dead drug-addicted brother probably has no clue as to what your father's doing, but he must die also because my son had to die for your father. It'll be done in such a way that your father will think his guy is coming after him. I want to see him sweat like the pig he is."

"You really are a monster, aren't you?"

"No. Your father is the monster, I'm the boogie man that kills the monsters."

TWENTY-ONE

Langley Op's Center

"Guardian, grab the brother and take him to The Barn."

"Roger, Skipper."

"We need to set this up so it looks like Williamson did it. I want to see this son of a bitch sweat and go to ground thinking he's being hunted by his own man. We'll inject each of them with a speed ball, put them in Teresa's car and drive them up to Skyline Drive in the Shenandoah Valley. We'll take a second car and run into them and make it look like they were run off the road. Then make it look like they drove over the cliff after being hit. We have to be careful there are no witnesses and make sure none of us get hurt doing it. I'll then go down the hill and shoot each one of them in the head like he did my family. Make it look like he did the same thing to Baker's family. I want to verify they're dead before anyone finds them. Merlin, can you rig something up for the accelerator that'll keep it wide open but not be found after the crash?"

"Sure Skipper, that should be an easy fix."

"Good. I'll do the shooting and then Merlin will rig the gas. I'll stand beside the car and throw it in gear and jump out of the way as it goes over the cliff. Everybody straight on this?"

"Roger, Skipper."

TWENTY-TWO

Franklin Cliffs Overlook – Skyline Drive

Shenandoah National Park

"Now that we have had a nice little ride and the drugs have had time to really take effect, it's time to get this show on the road. Merlin, how long before you're ready?"

"About ten minutes, Skipper."

"Ok. Let's get everyone into position. They're pretty much zombies at this point. Put the brother in the back, hubby will be driving and put her in the passenger seat. They would have to be driving a friggin Mercedes 300SD. Damn thing is like a tank. At least it's not the turbo diesel, thank God."

Travis and his team get the cars set up and Boomer gets in the second car. Boomer backs off about a quarter of a mile. Travis gives the word and Boomer accelerates and heads for the other car. Just as Boomer gets to the car, he swerves, and side swipes the other car. Boomer then drives the other car out of the way.

"Good to go when you are, Skipper."
"Ok. Clear south?"
"Green light."
"Clear north?"
"Green light."
"Get out and slam the car into gear. Man, that was close!!! Took off like a bat outta hell!! No way anyone's walking away from that. Everybody clear out and come back around and get me. I'm going down to make sure we're done."
"Roger, Skipper. How long do you need?"
"The Visitor's Center is about one and a half clicks south. Meet me there in about 45 minutes."

Travis eased his way down the hillside to the crash site. The car was burning, and Travis looked inside and shot each one in the head as planned. He decided they would have to use dental records to identify the bodies. He was satisfied that everything was to his liking and took off headed south at about a seven-minute mile pace. He would get there in plenty of time to get rested before being picked up by the team.

Travis arrived at the Visitor's Center about 12 minutes later. The team would follow in ten minutes. Travis sat down and started planning what needed to happen next. Travis was deep in thought when the team showed up to pick him up.

"Everything ok, Skipper?"
"Yeah, everything looks good."
They took the second car with them, found a deserted field on the outskirts of DC, and set it on fire.

TWENTY-THREE

Langley Op's Center

"Let's get some rest men. It'll probably take a couple of days for the coroner to be able to identify the bodies. We've got a lot to go over and a lot of planning to do. Rest and spend time contacting the families. You men, as always, performed above and beyond as the professionals you are. Thank you for your professionalism and dedication to team, country and me. We'll reassemble at 13:00 tomorrow. Dismissed."

"Rise and shine gentlemen. It's early am and time to get this show on the road. Meet in 15 in the Op's Center."

"Roger that, Skipper. The Op's Center in 15."

"Men, I have decided to let Baker find out about his family and give him a few days to do the right thing or we'll do it for him. If he doesn't take his own life, then I'll take him down and humiliate him in the public's eyes. I'm not going to take him out like I had planned on doing. I want him to think about this for the rest of his miserable life. I want him looking over his shoulder if the wind starts blowing or he hears a whisper. Let's get to work putting together a story that can be leaked to the press if he doesn't do the right thing. I want it tight and concise with supporting documents in his own handwriting and backed up by other paperwork that the bastard can't wiggle his ass out of. We want to use the intel his daughter had on him, but not the items we have on the other members of the House and Senate. That will be used at a later date. Now let's get moving and have our ducks in a row when the shit hits the fan."

Travis and the team set out to get their story together and have it ready to go. Seven hours later they're finished and ready.

"All right boys, now we sit back and wait for the news to break about his family. I want him watched like a hawk when it does."

"All right men, the coroner has his findings and is supposed to be making the announcement in a news conference in five minutes. Let's get the TV on and watch what happens when the news is released."

"NBC has just received word from the coroner's office of Washington County that a press conference is being broadcast and we are covering it live. Let's go live to that news conference now."

"Ladies and gentlemen, it's with a heavy heart that I must announce that the daughter, son and son-in-law of Senator William Baker and his wife Joanne were the victims of a murder that happened on Skyline Drive at the Franklin Cliffs Overlook. It appears that the car they were riding in was forced off the road and down the overlook. The car burst into flames. The bodies were identified using dental records. It was found at autopsy that each had been shot in the head once. This is a brutal and heinous crime. Our hearts and prayers go out to the family of Senator Baker and his wife. The Senator and his wife are dealing with this tragedy in private for now and will be making an announcement at a later date. Thank you and that is all."

"All right men, now we wait and see if he does the right thing or if we have to do it for him. Anybody want to lay odds that he goes to the President seeking revenge for this? He won't do the right thing, but we will. I feel truly sorry for his wife. I bet she has no clue what's going on with her husband."

"Breaking news. NBC news has just been informed that Senator William Baker is going to meet with President James Carpenter in the Oval Office at the White House tomorrow. Now back to your regular news."

"I told you he would. I have to go see Turner. I have to get to President Carpenter. Director Turner, can you get me in to see President Carpenter?"

"I think I can arrange that. It might take me a day or two."

TWENTY-FOUR

Oval Office – The White House

"Mr. President, thank you for seeing me today."

"Not a problem, Bill. I want you to know that Roslynn and I are so sorry to hear about what happened to your family. How's Joanne holding up?"

"Not good, Mr. President. It's a struggle for her to even get out of bed."

"I can't even imagine what you must be going through. If there's anything we can do for you, just ask."

"I'm glad you feel that way, Mr. President. I have an idea who may have done this. I need you to get me a team to go after this son of a bitch. He threatened me and my family before and I didn't take him seriously. That was a mistake on my part. I don't want him caught; I want him dead. Can you make that happen Mr. President?"

"I'll check into it and get back to you in the next few days, Bill. I have a meeting tomorrow with the Director of the CIA."

"Thank you, Mr. President."

Senator Baker leaves the White House thinking he'll be able to get the President to solve his problem for him and he'll come out smelling like a rose. He couldn't be further from the truth.

TWENTY-FIVE

Oval Office – The White House

"Thank you for seeing me today, Mr. President."

"Not a problem, Peter. I had a meeting yesterday with Bill Baker and I was going to call you anyway. You made it sound urgent. What is it you need, Peter?"

"Mr. President, I brought someone with me that you've met before. This is Travis Bones, Sir."

"Yes, I remember. How are you Sergeant Bones?"

"I'm doing fine, Mr. President. I'm not a Sergeant anymore, though. I work for Director Turner now, Sir."

"That's good, Mr. Bones. Now Peter, what is it you need to see me about?"

"Actually Mr. President, it has to do with Senator Baker. We have some documents you need to see, Sir. What did Senator Baker want, if you don't mind my asking, Sir?"

"Not at all, Peter. He wanted to know if I could get a team to take care of a problem he has. He seems to think he knows who murdered his children."

"He does, Mr. President. The guy works for the Senator. But not how you may think. You need to look at the documents I mentioned earlier, Sir, and it will all become clear for you as to why he asked you that."

"Ok, let's have a look at the documents."

The President spends some time going through all the documents. He gets up and walks over to the fireplace in the Oval Office and stares into the fireplace with a look the director had never seen on the President before.

"Hmmmm. Is this for real, Peter?"

"Yes, Sir it is. Senator Baker had Travis's family killed to try to keep his dealings with the cartels a secret, but he grossly underestimated Travis. That's how Travis came to work for me, Sir."

"You actually saw him in Columbia with Escobar?"

"Yes, Sir, I did."

"What do you think we should do about this, Peter?"

"Mr. President, we already have documents and proof ready to be released to the press anonymously. Things he can't talk his way out of this time, Sir."

"All right Peter, I trust you and Travis to do the right thing. Travis, I'm so sorry for the sacrifice you and your family have made for this country. We are forever in your debt."

"Thank you, Mr. President, that means a lot coming from you personally, Sir. We'll make this right and see that justice is done with no blow back to you, Sir."

"And to think that I would have helped him, not knowing what he was doing, trying to cover his own ass."

"Yes Sir, Mr. President. That's what a rodent like him does. Covers his own ass at the expense of those around him. And goes home and lays his head down like nothing happened and sleeps well, Sir."

"All right gentlemen, I leave this in your hands. Is his wife involved in all of this?"

"As far as we can tell she has no idea what her husband has been up to at all. I really feel sorry for her. First losing her family, and now she will lose him. It's truly tragic for her."

"Yes, it is Travis. Yes, it is."

TWENTY-SIX

Langley Op's Center

"All right men, the President is on board with us handling the release of information to the press anonymously. What's the latest intel on Baker?"

"He has scheduled a press conference for 15:30 tomorrow afternoon. I guess he's trying to wait for the President to get back to him."

"I'll talk to Director Turner and see if we can set it up to look like the President has the CIA on board and watch as he thinks his ass is covered and in the clear."

Travis talks to Director Turner and brings him up to speed on his plan. The director agrees with Travis and makes the call. "Senator Baker, this is CIA Director Peter Turner."

"Yes Director, I take it the President has talked to you?"

"Yes Sir, he has. The President said that you may have an idea who did this to your family?"

"Yes Director, he threatened me and my family not long ago and I stupidly did not take him seriously. I know I should've had him checked out, but I doubt we would have uncovered his intentions then. These sorts of people never let on to what their plans are beforehand as I'm sure you're aware of."

"All too well, Senator. Do you have a name or any information about this man?"

"Yes, I do, Director. His name is Don Williamson. He's a dishonorably discharged Navy S.E.A.L. with an axe to grind against the government and apparently me in particular."

"Do you know why he singled you and your family out?"

"I'm afraid I have no idea."

"Have you ever had any personal dealings with this man?"

"No, I've never met or heard of this man before he threatened me and my family."

"All right Senator, I'll have my people get on this and I'll keep you informed when we find him and take care of the problem. Do you and your wife want a protection detail assigned to you?"

"That won't be needed. I have already hired private security."

"All right, I'll call as soon as we have confirmation, Senator."

"Thank you for your speed and help in handling this matter, Director."

"Senator, before I go, how did he contact you before? Was it by phone or letter?"

"He first sent a letter to my office, then a few days later he called my office and I talked directly to him."

"Do you still have the letter?"

"No, it was thrown out with all the junk mail from my office the day after it came in."

"All right Senator, thank you. What did he say to you when you talked to him?"

"He said that my family and I would pay dearly for what the government had done to him."

"Anything else?"

"No, he hung up after he said this."

"Ok Senator, I'll be in touch soon."

"Did you hear that, Travis?"

"Yes, Sir, I did. My question is how did he come up with the name because Williamson would not have put it in the letter or told him over the phone? He had to have known him to get the name. Got ya! Of course, we know he did know him, but that proves it and he has nothing to prove otherwise. I'll make arrangements to meet with a reporter and leak the information after his press conference."

William E. Boone

TWENTY-SEVEN

Press Conference for Senator Baker

Napa, California

NBC Breaking News. "Good afternoon, we are interrupting your regular programming to go live to the press conference with Senator Baker."

"Good afternoon and thank you for coming. I wish to thank everyone for their thoughts and prayers for my family and I. As you know, we lost our son, daughter and son-in law. This was a heinous crime. I understand, or should I say, I have heard through the grapevine so to speak, that there is a suspect in this case. I don't know why this person has singled my family out and done this to us. I apologize for the absence of my wife; she is having a very hard time with all that has happened. I wish to thank everyone involved for respecting our privacy. Tomorrow we'll be having the memorial service for our family. I ask that you understand that the service will be family and close friends only. I wish that we could accommodate those of you who would want to come, but I feel at this time that it would be best for my family to have this as family and close friends only. I hope that this case is brought to a conclusion very quickly and that the person or people responsible for this heinous act are brought to swift and extreme justice."

Travis and his team watched the news conference and understandably were pissed at what the senator had to say and how he said it. Travis found it hard to believe the arrogance and bravado of this man. Travis slowly walked into the other room and swore to himself that the senator would go down hard when the plan was set into motion. For now, Travis had to figure out how he and the team would handle the funeral coverage tomorrow.

TWENTY-EIGHT

First Presbyterian Church of Napa

Travis knew he could not be at the church for the funeral, as Baker knew his face. He knew if Baker saw him there, he would figure out it was Travis and not Williamson who had done this to his family. This would ruin the plan they had in place to bring him down.

Director Turner walks up to Travis, who's in deep thought.

"Travis, what have you got in mind to cover the funeral?"

"We both know I can't be there and I'm not willing to put my team in there as we don't know for sure if Baker gave up any information to the cartels. I would like to have one of your men go in and let Baker know that you sent him to keep an eye out during the funeral. He'll be wired of course so we can listen to what happens. I think it would be good for you to go also, Sir. Make him think everything is ok. Tell him you have an update for him after the funeral is over."

"What do you want me to tell him?"

"Tell him that you've traced Williamson to California and that's why you and your men are here today. To make sure he's safe and to be ready when you pin down an exact location on him."

"That Travis, sounds like a plan."

Travis sits back in the van and watches and listens as Director Turner goes into the funeral and talks to Baker. Turner's man is stationed next to the family so Travis can listen to the wife and get any idea if she knows anything or not. Travis still believes she has no clue as to what her husband is up to or what's about to happen to him.

Travis sits back and listens as the funeral begins. He has a heavy heart as he drifts back and remembers Sarah and Jamie's funeral. He is lost in remembrance as he realizes the funeral is ending. He listens as Turner goes up to Baker and tells him that they think they have a location locked down for Williamson. Baker seems almost giddy. He thinks his problem is about to go away. Turner tells him that they will accompany Baker home and stay with him until they're sure, and everything is wrapped up. Baker thanks him and they leave the funeral headed home. Travis follows them at a safe distance until they get home. Travis parks the van out of sight and waits for Turner to show up at the van.

"What's the plan now, Travis?"

"Now we call the President and get an arrest warrant signed for this piece of crap."

"What will the charges be?"

"Treason to start with and we'll add more at a later date. Have the President get it done asap. In the meantime, you go in and tell Baker we have Williamson surrounded and are waiting for the warrant to arrive to execute. He has hostages and we can't take him out till we get the hostages out. At least the warrant part won't be a lie. I'll send the warrant in when it arrives."

"Ok, Travis. Do you want to be there when we serve it?"

"No, I'll come out after it's been served. I want him to know it was me that got his ass."

"Ok. I'll call the President and have the warrant expedited. Travis, I'll personally serve the warrant on him."

"Thank you, Director. That means a lot to me."

Travis waits in the van. He thinks back to what Baker has done to his family and he feels the rage building inside. He must not let the rage take over now. He must stay in control of his emotions. If the rage takes over now, it will destroy everything that he has worked to accomplish. That can't happen now. Not at this stage of the game. Travis closes his eyes and thinks about all the good times with Sarah and Jamie. After about five minutes, Travis regains his composure and is in control once again of his emotions. Once again Sarah and Jamie have reached out from the grave to make things right again in Travis's world.

As Travis opened his eyes, an agent showed up at the van with the warrant for Senator Baker.

Travis instructed him to go to the house and ask for Director Turner. "Give him the warrant and make sure you're outside away from everybody when you give it to him. I don't want anyone screwing the pooch on this one. I want it clean and concise, understand?"

"Yes, Sir."

"Good, now go."

Travis put on the head set so he could listen to everything as it happened. He watched as the agent went to the front door and waited for Turner. Turner shows up and the agent hands him the warrant. Turner looks at the van and turns and walks inside. Travis thought to himself, *here we go*.

Turner walks up to Senator Baker. "Senator, could I have a word in private?"

"Certainly Peter, good news I hope." They go into the senator's study. Turner looks at the senator.

"I don't think this is exactly what you're looking for, Bill. Senator William Baker, I have a warrant for your arrest."

"What in the Hell are you talking about, a warrant for my arrest?"

"Yes, Sir."

"On what charges?"

"Treason to start with, Senator. Treason against your country."

"That's about the stupidest thing I've ever heard. What can you possibly come up with that could even remotely be called treason?"

"How about you being on the payroll of the largest drug cartel in the world, Senator."

"That has to be the most ridiculous thing I've ever heard. You actually think I would be involved in something like that, Peter?"

"Yes Bill, I do. I have documents proving it."

"You can't be serious."

"Bill, please turn around and place your hands on your head. You are under arrest."

"You've just signed your career death warrant, Peter. I'll see you're run out of Washington and become the laughingstock of law enforcement."

"Bill, your days of running rough shod over people comes to an end here and now. Turn around and place your hands on your head or I'll do it for you."

Baker slowly turns and does as Turner tells him. Turner places the handcuffs on Baker.

"Is this really necessary, Peter?"

"Yes, it is Senator. Treason is a very serious crime and you must be dealt with in a serious manner. You may as well get used to it because it only gets worse from here for you." Turner walks the senator out of the house.

When they step outside, Travis is waiting with a big smile on his face. "Surprised to see me, Senator?" Baker's eyes widen as he sees Travis standing there. "Didn't expect to see me again, did you? Surprise, I'm still here. It'll be a cold day in Hell before you and your kind stop me, Senator. Now you're going to pay and pay dearly for what you did to my family. I'll personally see to it that you're never able to do this to anybody else ever again, you piece of shit!! I have enough evidence against you to bury your sorry ass. By the time I'm through with you, you'll be lucky if you ever see daylight again. You had better enjoy it for what little time you can. Turner, get this piece of shit out of here before I decide to save the taxpayers a lot of money and finish the job myself." Travis spins around and walks off before he does what he really wants to do to Baker. God knows it takes all of Travis's willpower not to finish the job right here, right now. As Travis walks away, a huge smile comes across his face and he actually finds himself laughing. He turns and looks at Turner and Baker and the expression on Baker's face makes Travis laugh even harder. Baker looks like somebody kicked him in the balls and told him he didn't hurt. Travis turns and walks off still laughing. He thinks to himself, *I got you, you son of a bitch. I got you*!!

TWENTY-NINE

Langley Op's Center

Travis thought to himself, *now the fun begins*. It had been a good day for Travis and a better day for America. One treasonous bastard is off the streets and behind bars where he should be. Travis would be sure to be at Baker's arraignment hearing. Travis would be damned if the senator, or should we say ex-senator, would get out on bail. He would make sure that didn't happen. He would also make sure that the judge was not on Baker's payroll.

Travis set about the task of going through the list of names of people on Baker's payroll or who owed him favors. He came across four judges that owed Baker favors. Travis called Turner. "Director, this is Travis. I found four judges names that owe Baker favors. Who's hearing Baker's arraignment?"

"Judge Allen Cromwell."

"We have to get the judge changed. Cromwell is one of the judges owing favors to Baker. It can't be Cromwell, Orson, Dawson or Bean. They all owe Baker favors for things he has done for them. I knew that sorry son of a bitch would try to get someone that owed him something to hear his arraignment."

"Good job, Travis. I'll make sure none of those judges hear the case."

"Thank you, Sir. I don't want this piece of shit getting out or trying to get it dismissed on a technicality."

"I'll personally see that doesn't happen."

Turner makes a call to the President.

"Mr. President, we have a problem."

"What's the problem?"

"The judge for Baker's hearing."

"What's the problem with the judge?"

"He owes favors to Baker, Sir."

"That could be a big problem. What do you suggest?"

"Well Sir, he has four judges that we know of who owe him favors, and we need to make sure that none of the four hear his arraignment."

"Ok, tell me the names and I'll make sure they have nothing to do with Baker's case."

"Those names are Cromwell, Orson, Dawson and Bean."

"Ok Peter, I'll make sure none of them get anywhere near this case."

"Thank you, Mr. President." Turner calls Travis to let him know that the President is taking care of the problem.

It's time for Travis to put his plan into action. Travis calls his source in the media. "Hello Bob. I have some information I think you might be interested in."

"And what might that be?"

"Senator William Baker."

"What has the good Senator done?"

"Do you know where Turkey Run Park is?"

"Yeah, why?"

"Meet me there in two hours at the last parking lot on Turkey Run Loop Road and I'll give you the story of a lifetime."

"Ok. I'll be there. Don't let me down."

"Oh, don't worry, I won't."

Travis sat in the parking lot waiting for his media source to get there. He thought about Sarah and Jamie. He could still smell Sarah's perfume in the car, and it made him wonder how long that would last. His heart ached for his wife and son, imagining how scared they must have been. He just hoped they were dead before the fire started. He would make sure that Williamson was not. He thought about how Sarah had taken his breath away the first time he saw her on their wedding day. How beautiful she was standing there in her wedding dress. He remembered the day that Jamie was born. How something that small and helpless could put so much love and joy in his heart. He remembered how his heart swelled with love and pride the first time Jamie told him he loved him. Now he thought about never being able to hear that again. Travis snapped back to reality when his source pulled in beside him.

"Hello, Bob. You ready to hear the story of a lifetime?"

"Hello, Travis, you really have my curiosity peaked. Knowing you, I'm sure it has to be juicy."

"I promise, you will have your mind blown completely before I'm through. I called you because I know you've been investigating Senator Baker. If you don't mind my asking, what got you started investigating Baker in the first place?"

"I heard from a reputable source that he was involved in some dubious activity."

"What kind of activity?"

"Bribery and controlling elections on all levels. Hell, from what I hear, he decides who wins and who losses."

"Well my friend, that's small potatoes compared to what I'm about to give you, and mine comes with documentation to back it up."

"I'm all ears, Buddy. Is this off the record or on?"

Travis considered this for a moment. He really wanted to say on the record, but he knew with his new situation, there was no way he could.

"This is going to be off the record from a reputable source."

"Ok, I'm good with that."

"Take a look at this and tell me what you think."

His source looked at the documents Travis had given him, and his smile grew bigger and his eyes got wider. "He has been arrested for treason?"

"Yes, he has, and as you can see, we have the documents to prove it."

"Damn!! I knew he was a crooked son of a gun, but damn."

"He was the one that caused the death of Sarah and Jamie."

"I was really sorry to hear about that Travis. I know how much you loved them. How are you handling things?"

"Better now. Now that I know the son of a bitch who caused it is going down. Hell, he even tried to get a judge that owes him a favor to hear his arraignment."

"You've got to be kidding me."

"I'm serious as a heart attack."

"You run this story and I'll keep you informed of any new evidence we come up with."

"You weren't kidding about this being the story of a lifetime. You just made my career. Why did you pick me?"

"One, because I know you're a good, reputable journalist who people believe. Second, I know you don't care much for the Senator. And three, I know you were already investigating him."

"Travis, I don't know how I'll ever be able to thank you for this."

"You can thank me by making sure the story gets out there and is told in the right way. I know you'll do this."

THIRTY

Langley Op's Center

Travis slept well last night for the first time since the death of his wife and son. He felt good about the fact that Baker was in jail, but Travis isn't an idiot. He knows that being the manipulative asshole Baker is, he'll be trying to run his kingdom from his jail cell. Travis knows he must come up with a plan to keep this from happening. Travis knows that Baker will be trying to get his lawyer and his cronies to get the charges dropped altogether, or at the very least, reduced to something that carries no jail time. Having friends in high places could result in this actually happening. Travis tries to put himself in Baker's place and come up with what kind of plan Baker may try to get going.

Travis calls the team together and lets them in on what he suspects. "All right guys, we know Baker's in jail. I also know that he'll be running his kingdom from his jail cell. He'll be digging up anything he or his cronies can come up with to get the charges dropped or reduced to no jail time. Start digging through all the intel we have and see if there's anything that he might even remotely use and make a list. I have to take a trip and I want answers when I get back."

Travis made a phone call and sets off for a meeting with Bob Masteson, the NBC News journalist to whom Travis has given the information. He arrives at Old Ebbitt Grill in DC, gets a table and waits for Bob to arrive. Travis knows Baker will call in every favor owed him to beat this. Bob arrives and sits down.

"Hello, Bob. Good to see you again. What's the word on the street about Baker?"

"Hey, Travis, not a lot right now. The story really hasn't come out yet."

"Speaking of such, when's the big reveal scheduled to hit?"

"Funny you should ask. The story's scheduled to hit at three this afternoon."

"That's fantastic. The sooner the better. Less time for Baker to come up with a plan and bullshit story. Are they featuring you in this breaking story?"

"Thanks to the information you gave me, yes, I'll be featured when it breaks. You'll never know how grateful I am that you gave it to me instead of someone else."

"I know and trust you and know that Baker can't get his hooks into you like he can with a lot of other journalists."

"Thank you for the words of praise, and I won't let you down Travis."

"That's why you were chosen, Bob. Is there any kind of talk behind the scenes about this?"

"A little bit so far. The word is that his lawyer will ask that the charges be dropped at the arraignment. He's not really expecting that to happen so I'm sure he's working on an alternate plan."

"I figure he'll try to get the charges reduced to something with no jail time. With the information you gave me and with what I'm coming out with later, he might find that hard to do."

"I've got my men pouring through every piece of intel we have. They're making a list of possible ways he might try to wiggle his way out of this and who he'll call to help. Hell, he has half of Capitol Hill in his pocket as far as owing him favors. Hell, it wouldn't surprise me if Carpenter himself didn't owe him favors. So far, he's been on our side. I'll be watching to see if that changes. I'll be watching very closely indeed. I need to get back. I look forward to your story at three. Make it good."

"I will. See you later, Travis."

Travis leaves and proceeds back to Langley. As Travis heads back, he comes up with an idea to slow down Baker's plan. He turns the car around and drives back to DC. He pulls up in front of the police headquarters and parks and goes inside. Travis shows his ID and requests to see the Chief. He's ushered back to Chief Robert Ludlum's office. "What can I do for you, Mr. Bones?"

"Hello, Chief Ludlum, I'm here to talk to you about Senator Baker."

"What does the CIA want to know about Senator Baker?"

"It's not what I need to know, Chief, it's about what I need you to do for the CIA about Senator Baker."

"And what might that be?"

"I need for you to restrict access to the Senator. That includes his lawyer and all government officials until after seven o'clock this evening."

"Mr. Bones, do you realize how many laws that breaks?"

"Yes Sir, I do. But your government is asking you for that favor. It must be done in a way that doesn't set off any alarms with the legal community. All I can say right now is that the government needs this block of time to have some things happen for the good of America, Sir."

"For the good of America? Are you kidding me?"

"No, Sir, I'm serious as a heart attack right now, Chief."

"So, let me get this straight. You want me to put the Senator on pretty much lock down until seven this evening, and all you have is for the good of America!!"

"Yes Sir, that's what I mean. I can make a phone call if you need me to, Sir."

"I don't think that will be necessary. I think we might be able to come to an agreement on this matter without involving anyone else."

"Thank you, Chief, I was hoping you would see it that way."

"You have your window of time. I don't want any more favors asked after this. Are we clear on that?"

"Yes, Sir. Thank you again, Chief."

Travis was glad the chief went along with his plan. Travis had no one to call. This was strictly his idea and he didn't think Turner would go along with it, and he knew damn well that the President sure as Hell wouldn't. At least he had his window of time to let the story leak out without Baker being able to dilute the story when it broke. He knew Bob would do one Hell of a job with the story. Travis drove back to Langley running scenarios through his mind about what to do next.

THIRTY-ONE

Langley Op's Center

Travis arrived back at Langley, turned the TV to the NBC News station, and waited for the breaking story to come on.

"This is NBC News with a breaking story out of Washington, DC. We are going live to our correspondent Bob Masteson in Washington. Bob."

"Thank you, Cory. Today is a sad day for America. Senator William Baker has been arrested on charges of treason against his country. More charges may be pending, but we know for sure that he's charged with treason. Senator Baker has stated publicly in numerous interviews that he's fighting the drug problem in America with the full resources of the Federal Government. We have found out from a source high in the government that Senator Baker is working with and taking payments from the drug cartels in Columbia. He's paving the way for millions of dollars in illegal drugs to pour into this country from Columbian Cartels. With his seat as Chairman of the Armed Services Committee, he has the power and influence to be able to circumvent the war on drugs and provide a way for the cartels to bring their drugs into this country. He has access to information regarding all the operations the government has going to fight the cartels, and is passing this information on to them so they can steer clear of any operations to hamper their bringing drugs into the country. The American citizens should be outraged that someone they duly elected to fight these cartels is using his power to help them instead."

"Bob, what other charges may be pending against the Senator?"

"Cory, my sources have told me that he could possibly be looking at extortion, bribery and possibly even murder charges. Just to name a few."

"Bob, what could the murder charges be about?"

"Cory, my sources have shown me documentation that some of the information Senator Baker passed along to the cartels, has directly resulted in the deaths of several military personnel as well as civilians. Apparently, the cartels sent money to Senator Baker and he in turn hired and arranged for hit squads to take out these people the cartels wanted removed."

"That's quite disturbing, Bob."

"Yes, it is Cory. Apparently, Senator Baker used his influence on Capitol Hill to call in favors to get these things done. I have also been informed by my source that other charges may be pending on other people involved by helping the Senator. We'll be keeping a close eye on events as they unfold,

Cory. This is Bob Masteson reporting from Washington, DC."

"Thank you, Bob. We'll be bringing developments in this story to you as they become available. This is Cory Stevens for NBC News. Thank you for watching and we now return you to regular programming."

Travis caught himself with a huge smile on his face. He knew he had chosen the right person to give the information to. Bob Masteson was like a bulldog with a new soup bone. It was his and he owned it, and no one was going to take it away from him. Travis smiles even bigger. Life is good at the moment.

THIRTY-TWO

Central Jail – Washington DC

Travis decided to go to DC and have a talk with Baker. He wanted Baker to know that he wasn't about to let him off the hook with just a slap on the wrist. His time in control was over. Now Travis held the cards of power and he would make sure Baker paid and paid dearly!

"Travis Bones to see Senator Baker."

"Yes Sir, Mr. Bones. What is the nature of your visit?"

"I'm here to see the Senator about the charges against him and the potential charges that might be filed."

"Yes Sir, I'll need to check with Chief Ludlum, Sir."

"I understand, officer."

"Chief Ludlum, I have a Mr. Travis Bones here to see Senator Baker."

"It's ok officer, let him in. Tell him to come by my office when he's done."

"Yes Sir, thank you, Sir. You may go in to see him, Mr. Bones. The Chief would like to see you when you're done."

"Thank you."

Travis makes his way back to solitary confinement where Senator Baker is separated from the general population. Travis arrives at Baker's cell and the guard opens the door. Baker's eyes get wide and he steps back against the wall.

"Hello, Baker."

"What the Hell are you doing here?"

"We're going to have a little talk about things so you know where I stand and just how fucked you really are."

"I have nothing to say to you."

"Oh, but I have quite a bit to say to you and you will listen. Hell, you can't get away. I have the proverbial captive audience. Your power doesn't work in here like it does on Capitol Hill. You're going to listen and listen well. Sit down, shut up and open your ears. You might have power and influence on The Hill, but here you don't have squat. You're facing a charge of treason. That's a hangable offense in this country. I have enough hard evidence against you to bury you for the rest of your life. Did you happen to catch the news last night?"

"No, no one has said anything about the news. Why?"

"Your story was told on the news last night, so now the whole country knows. You've become the laughingstock of the government. Not to mention there's a whole nation out there pissed off at you right now. Treason is just the tip of the iceberg. If you're smart, you'll take the treason charge and shut up. If you don't, you'll be charged with extortion, bribery and murder among other things. You've already disgraced yourself in the eyes of the country. You'll be an even bigger disgrace if you try to fight the treason charge. Your wife is already in hiding from the public. How much do you want her to suffer? Haven't you done enough to her already? Your own man has taken your family away from you. Do you want him coming after her too?"

Travis knew this was a lie, but he needed Baker to believe it for now. Maybe he would tell him the truth before they hung his ass. But then again, maybe not. After what Baker had cost him personally, he didn't care what Baker thought. The more Baker worried about Williamson, the better for him and the case. Travis knew Williamson was far away from DC, but Baker needed to think he was close by and dangerous.

"You need to plead guilty to treason and be done or I'll personally see to it that as many charges as possible are filed against you."

"Do you really think I'm just going to roll over without a fight?"

"If you know what's good for you, you will. I can and will make your life and career a living Hell for you. The choice is yours. I already have you in jail. Don't think I'm not capable of doing what I say I will. Do you even care what your wife thinks? Does she not mean anything to you? If you've one ounce of compassion and feeling, you'll do what's right for her. She's the one left to face the public after you're gone. And you will be gone. Not in jail, but gone from this earth. This I promise you. Any way you look at it, your ass is mine!! You think about it and have your lawyer give me a call. If he's smart, he'll tell you the same thing I just did. Save the taxpayers some money and plead guilty."

Travis turns and walks away from Baker's cell. He knows Baker will fight this thing, but maybe, just maybe, he'll think about his wife. Travis heads to the chief's office.

"You wanted to see me, Chief?"

"Yes, I did Mr. Bones. Might I ask what you were talking about with the Senator?"

"Sure Chief, I was simply informing him that it would be in his best interest to plead guilty to treason and be done. I told him to think about his wife instead of himself for a change. She's the one who's going to have to live with all this long after he's dead and gone."

"Well, you have a valid point there, Mr. Bones. Did he seem receptive to the idea?"

"Please call me Travis and no, he wasn't at all receptive to the idea. I told him to have his lawyer call me. Hopefully, he'll listen to him and hopefully his lawyer is smart enough to know that this is the best deal he'll get. I'll personally be there when they hang his ass. Pardon my French."

"Well, let's hope for the best and expect the worst."

"Very well put, Chief. I couldn't have said it any better myself. Anything else, Chief?"

"No, I think that about wraps it up."

"Thanks again for last night, Chief. I really appreciate what you did."

"Why I have no idea what you're talking about, Travis."

Travis and the chief both laugh, and Travis turns and walks out of the chief's office still laughing. Travis can only hope that Baker and his lawyer make the right choice. Travis heads back to Langley and tells Turner that he needs a few days to find a place to stay. The Op's Center isn't his idea of home, and that's where Travis has been staying since coming to the CIA.

THIRTY-THREE

Somewhere in Washington DC

Travis decided to find a diner somewhere and a phone book so he could look up realtors. He stopped at several phone booths before he finally found one that had a phone book. He knew it was wrong, but he took the phone book just the same.

He found a diner that looked good and stopped. He went inside, ordered breakfast, settled in the booth and started looking at ads for realtors. His breakfast came and he started eating as he looked. He hated shopping for realtors. He had no idea who was good and who wasn't. Just as he was about to give up in frustration, the waitress came by to fill his coffee and saw him looking at realtors' names.

"I'm sorry, but I couldn't help but notice that you're looking at realtors. If you're looking, I happen to know a good one you should talk to."

"And who would that be?"

"I have a friend who's a realtor and she represents a lot of houses. Are you looking in the DC area or somewhere else?"

"I'm looking around the DC area. What's her name?"

"Claire, Claire Sullivan. She works for Sullivan and Associates. You should give her a call. Tell her Tammy sent you."

"Thank you, Tammy. Do you have her number?"

"Sure, I'll write it down for you. I'll write mine down for you also."

"Thank you. What's your last name, Tammy?"

"Oh, it's Kennedy. No relation to THE Kennedys. I get off at two if you wanted to know."

"Thank you, but I'm going to be busy the next few days looking for a house."

"Oh, yeah, sure. I understand."

"Maybe we could meet for drinks after I get my housing situation fixed."

"Yeah, that would be great."

They both smiled and Tammy went on her way to help other customers. Travis thought to himself, it's just a bit too early after losing his family to start having drinks and going out. He didn't want to hurt her feelings, so he played along. Travis knew that at six two and being in good shape with brown hair and blue eyes, he attracted some looks, but he just wasn't ready for anything right now.

Travis called Claire and told her what he was looking for. He made an appointment for later in the morning to meet and go over some properties. Travis finished his meal and paid the bill. He told Tammy goodbye and headed out to meet Claire.

"Hello. You must be Claire."

"Yes, I am, and you must be Travis. Tammy called and said you were headed this way. She described you to a tee."

"Tammy seems like a very sweet girl. Now, what have you got for me to look at?"

"I have several for you. I only have two that are on the water like you said you liked. One is a rather large house with water access and then I have one that sits on the river. It's smaller but has more land."

"Let's look at that one first."

"Ok. You can ride with me if you like."

"That would be fine. Shall we?"

Claire and Travis head out to look at the property. As they're riding, Claire is describing the house and grounds to Travis. The more he hears about the property, the more he likes what he hears. He's actually looking forward to getting there and seeing it for himself. They arrive and Travis immediately likes what he sees.

"This property sits directly on the Potomac River. It's five acres and has a wall around the entire property. There's a gate in the back wall leading to a private boat dock. It has a full security system. Two bedrooms, two and a half baths, living room, dining room with an island kitchen. It has an office and a den. Hardwood floors with tile in the kitchen and baths."

"The more you tell me the more I like it. Let's go inside and look around."

They went inside. Claire showed Travis all around the house and grounds outside along with the boat dock and boat. Travis was truly impressed and knew that he had found what he was looking for. He didn't need to look at anything else. He was home.

"And what would it take for me to own this piece of heaven?"

"Only $225,000. That includes everything."

"How much deposit would you need?"

"Ten percent would hold it."

Travis knew he should try to negotiate the price, but he didn't want to risk losing it to someone else for a few dollars. This place just felt like home and he wanted it.

"Ok, let's get the ball rolling on this."

"You don't want to look at anything else?"

"Nope, I'm ready to pull the trigger on this one now. How soon can you have the paperwork ready to be signed?"

"A couple of days and you should be ready to sign and move in."

"Make it happen, the sooner the better."

Travis felt for the first time in months that his life was starting to resemble something like normal. This was a good feeling for Travis. Travis got back to Langley and made some phone calls to have his things shipped and to get the money set up for signing.

Just as Travis was starting to relax and unwind, he received a call from Ben Phillips, Baker's lawyer.

"What can I do for you, Mr. Phillips?"

"I called to inform you that Senator Baker, after talking with you, has decided to take you up on your offer and not face further charges that he believes you can and will bring against him, but under one condition."

"And what might that condition be, Mr. Phillips?"

"That you promise to see to it that his wife doesn't suffer any repercussions for the actions of her husband."

"You can tell Baker that's one deal I guarantee will happen."

"We have a deal then, Mr. Bones?"

"We have a deal, Mr. Phillips."

Travis hangs up the phone and couldn't believe what just happened. He never thought in a million years that Baker would give up this easy. He has to talk to Turner right away. Travis picks up the phone and dials Turner's number.

"Hello Director, this is Travis."

"Yes Travis, what can I do for you?"

"You're not going to believe the conversation I just had with Baker's lawyer."

"What did Phillips have to say?"

"I went by to see Baker in jail and had a talk with him. I told him to have his lawyer call me after they talked."

"And what did this visit of yours consist of, Travis?"

"Just letting him know that I was going to bury him and there wasn't a damn thing he could do about it. I told him he would be wise to take the treason charge and plead guilty or I would bury him under a mountain of other charges and to think about his wife instead of himself for a change."

"I see. And what did Phillips have to say about that?"

He said that if I guarantee his wife wouldn't suffer the wrath of the press over what he had done, that Baker would plead guilty to treason and be done."

"And what did you tell him?"

"That this was one deal I could guarantee I would make happen. He said we have a deal. Baker will plead guilty to treason."

"That's outstanding work, Travis. That makes it easy for the rest to be prosecuted. This is really fantastic. I probably would have gone about it differently, but you got the job done. Good work, Travis. I knew taking you on would be a good idea."

"Thank you, Sir. Now I'll take a few days and get settled into my new place."

"That's fine, Travis. You've definitely earned it."

THIRTY-FOUR

New House on the River

Travis made arrangements to spend the next few days getting moved into his new place. He called Bob Masteson and let him know what Phillip's had said. He also watched as Bob went on TV and informed the world of what was happening. He then spent time checking on Baker's wife from a distance. Now it was time to move in.

Travis moved his things in and started unpacking. The first box he opened had pictures of Sarah and Jamie in it. Travis sat down and went through the pictures until he felt the tears streaming down his face. He hadn't even realized that he was crying until now. He picked up his favorite picture with both Sarah and Jamie in it and started walking around the house showing them the new place. This made him happy as he felt like they were there with him. Travis spent the next four hours talking to and showing Sarah and Jamie the house and all it entailed.

Travis spent the next two days getting the house set up and all the things put in place. He spent time each day talking to Sarah and Jamie. This made him feel warm inside and it felt like they were a part of the move. He knew this was crazy, but it made his life sane and livable for now. He knew that if anyone heard him, they would think he had gone crazy. This made him laugh at himself. Who knows, maybe he had gone just a little bit crazy. Travis decided it was time to try out the boat. It was a 1980 Bayliner Ciera Family Cruiser. It had a cabin with a bed and a galley. Full radio equipment and a sky bridge.

Travis didn't feel like going out alone so he decided to call Tammy. Maybe they could talk, and he could explain things without hurting her feelings. Tammy said she got off at two and would very much like to join him for an outing on the boat. Travis gave her directions to the house and she said she would be there at three. Travis made the boat ready and waited on Tammy to arrive.

Tammy arrived at three sharp and Travis showed her around the house. She seemed truly interested and was glad that Travis had found such a beautiful place. They talked about Claire and how Tammy knew her. It felt good to have someone to talk too. Travis felt like he and Tammy could be friends. She was easy to talk to and she had a genuine interest in what Travis had to say. He was glad he had called.

They made their way out to the boat and Tammy was very impressed by the size and luxury of the boat. Travis explained that it had come with the house and that until now, he had not had time to take it out. Travis started the engine and they left the dock for a nice river cruise.

"So, Travis, I see that you have a wedding ring on. Where's your wife?"

"She and my son were killed in a car accident in California. They were going to see some friends in San Diego, and they were run off the road and went down an embankment and the car caught on fire. They never had a chance."

"Oh my God. Travis I'm so sorry. When did this happen?"

"A couple of months ago."

"Then it's still fresh in your mind. I'm so very sorry to hear that. You must still be struggling with coming to terms with it."

"Thank you, and yes I am. I find myself talking to them all the time. I know that makes me sound like I'm crazy, but it really does help."

"I know what you mean. I lost my mother to cancer a couple of years ago and I still find myself talking to her when I have a problem. You don't sound crazy at all. It sounds like you loved them very much."

"They were my world and the reason I got up in the morning. I still find it hard to believe they're gone."

"Anytime you need to talk you can just call me."

"Thank you, Tammy, I just might take you up on that from time to time."

"I would really enjoy that, Travis. Now I understand why you said what you did when I gave you my number at the diner. I feel like such a fool."

"Don't feel that way. You had no way of knowing what was going on. I think we can be good friends and help each other out when we're having a hard time with things. What do you think?"

"I think that sounds wonderful and I would be honored to be that kind of friend to you."

"Good. Then it's settled. Now let's see what this baby can do."

With that, Travis moves the throttle forward and they take off. They laugh, knowing they both have just found a new friend. As the day winds down into evening, they realize they're hungry. Travis turns the boat toward home and they decide to get something to eat.

After getting back to the house, they go into DC and grab some dinner. They end up at Old Ebbitt Grill and have a wonderful time. After dinner, Tammy tells Travis that she needs to be getting home as she has to be at work early. Travis thanks her for a wonderful afternoon and heads back home with a light heart and a smile on his face.

THIRTY-FIVE

Napa California

Travis takes the CIA's private jet to Napa County Airport. He needs to check in on Baker's wife and keep his promise so Baker would keep his. He lands at the airport and rents a car to drive to the Baker's home.

Travis arrives at the Baker's home only to find that the street has become a mini city with reporters from every major news agency parked up and down the street. Travis needs to come up with a plan to get rid of the reporters.

Travis walks up to some of the reporters and asks what's going on. They tell him they're waiting on Senator Baker's wife to come out. Travis looks at them and tells them they're wasting their time. Baker's wife is staying somewhere in DC so she can see her husband. They ask Travis how he knows this. Travis tells them he works for the government and saw her there this morning. The reporters turn and head to their vehicles and leave to talk to their respective agencies. Travis waits for them to go and then heads to the front door of the Baker home. Travis knocks on the door and the housekeeper asks who it is through the door. Travis tells her that he's with the government and needs to talk to Mrs. Baker - that it's very important. In a moment the door opens, and Travis is face to face with Baker's wife. He explains that he needs to talk to her. She invites Travis in and she asks him how he got rid of all the reporters and he tells her what he told them. She laughs and said she wished she had thought of that.

"Mrs. Baker, my name is Travis Bones and I work with the government. I made a promise to your husband that I intend to keep. I need to have you come with me so I can keep the reporters away from you and keep you safe."

"Where on earth can you possibly take me that they will not find me?"

"To start with, we'll go to the house at Big Bear Lake. From there I'll be able to move you around until the reporters get tired of chasing you, and until I can come up with a permanent plan to make them leave you alone."

"Do you think that will work for now?"

"I just bought us at least a couple of day's head start. I'll pull into the garage and put you in the back. You'll have to lay down under a blanket until we get out on the road. Then you can sit up."

"Isn't that a little cloak and dagger?"

"It's that or I can leave, and they will come back."

"Very well. I really can't take much more of the hounding they've been doing."

Travis pulls the car into the garage and waits long enough to make sure no one is watching. He takes Mrs. Baker out to the car, lays her in the back floorboard, and covers her with a blanket. They leave the residence without incident and Travis heads for the highway. Once they're well away from the house and Travis no longer sees any news vehicles, he pulls over, helps Mrs. Baker out of the floorboard, and puts her up front with himself. They drive in silence to Big Bear Lake. Travis pulls the car into the garage and shuts the door and goes upstairs and checks the house. He looks out the window and sees a glint of light. That's either from a gun sight or a camera lens. Travis figures it's the latter. Must be some reporter with a telephoto lens some distance away. New game plan.

Travis goes back downstairs and tells Mrs. Baker what he saw. Change of plans. Travis tells Mrs. Baker that they're going to the airport and have the plane meet them there.

"Where are we going now?"

"I have a house in DC on the Potomac River. No one will be looking for you there. You can stay with me there and I can make sure you're safe and away from prying eyes."

"Why would you do that for me?"

"I made a promise and I intend to keep it."

"What kind of promise and why?"

"Mrs. Baker, I made a promise to your husband. I'm not a fan of his, but I gave him my word I would keep you safe."

"Why don't you like my husband?"

"Because your husband is responsible for the deaths of my wife and son and four Marines trying to protect them."

"My Bill would never be involved with anything like that!"

"He was. Your husband is charged with treason because he's in bed with the drug cartels. I personally witnessed him in Columbia working with the cartels to bring millions of dollars worth of drugs into this country."

"He would never do anything that you're suggesting."

"He's also responsible for your children's deaths. Because he was so power hungry and greedy, the people he dealt with had your children killed. You're lucky they didn't come after you."

"If this is true, why are you helping me?"

"Because I told your husband if he pleads guilty to treason, I wouldn't go after him for extortion, bribery and murder. I also told him I would make sure you're not harassed by the media. You do understand that treason is a hangable offense in the United States, don't you?"

"Yes, I know that. But why would he do something like that?"

"Because he wanted power and money. His greed took over his common sense."

"Why would he do something that would put his family in danger?"

"Because power became more important to him than family."

"Bill would never put power or anything else before his family. He loves me and his children more than anything in this world."

"So tell me you haven't seen changes in his behavior as he gains more and more power."

"Of course I have. With power comes more responsibility and pressure."

"Did you ever stop to think about how he kept gaining more and more power on Capital Hill?"

"I just assumed that he was working harder and gaining the respect of his peers."

"Do you ever listen to yourself? Gaining the respect of your peers does not give you the kind of power he yielded on the Hill. Hell, half of the people on Capital Hill owed him favors. That doesn't come with respect. That comes from having some very powerful friends that intimidate people and have very deep pockets. Just think about it for a minute. How could he wield that kind of power without some sort of backing?"

"Oh my God. I'm so sorry that you and your family had to suffer because of his selfish wishes. I guess he never really cared about me or his family."

"His caring about you is how I got him to agree to this."

"So, what happens now?"

"He will be found guilty of treason and hanged. The legacy he worked so hard to build will be destroyed. You will be left to pick up the pieces and carry on. Do you have any idea how much he's worth?"

"No. We never discussed anything to do with finances."

"When he dies, you'll be worth 40 to 50 million dollars - a lot of which came from illegal dealings with the cartels and shady dealings on Capitol Hill."

"Oh my God. I had no idea."

"You'll be a very rich lady."

"I promise you that I'll use some of that money to do good and try to atone for some of the things my husband did."

Travis pulls out of the garage and heads for the airport to meet the plane. Once on the plane back to DC, Travis can at last relax.

He only hopes that Mrs. Baker will keep her word and use some of that money to do good.

THIRTY-SIX

Washington DC

The jet arrives safely in DC and Travis takes Mrs. Baker to his home. She's been very quiet on the flight back and on the ride to the house. Travis can only imagine what's going through her mind. He knows that what he revealed to her probably has her physically and emotionally in shock. When they arrive at Travis's home, he takes her inside and shows her around. He shows her the room that she'll be using and excuses himself. She asks him to stay for a moment.

"Mr. Bones, you've been gracious enough to open your home to me after everything my husband did to you. You'll never know just how grateful I am for that. I meant what I said to you and I want you to be the very first thing I take care of. I'm forever grateful to you for being honest with me. Most people just tell me what they think I want to hear. You were brutally honest, and I really appreciate that. The first thing I'd like to do with the money is set up a scholarship fund in your wife and son's name and fund it every year at a school of your choosing."

"Mrs. Baker, that's a truly lovely idea. I would be very honored to have that happen. Thank you! Please call me Travis."

"Ok Travis. I would be honored to do that for you and your family. If it's not inappropriate, could you show me pictures of your family?"

"It would be my pleasure."

Travis proceeds to show Mrs. Baker pictures of Sarah and Jamie. He tells her stories about them as the pictures come up. He tells her about what was happening when the picture was taken. This lasted well into the night. Mrs. Baker goes off to bed and Travis sits back and thinks about what has happened today. Suddenly he is very tired.

Travis gets up the next morning and finds Mrs. Baker already up. Travis tells her he'll be gone for several days and isn't sure when he'll be back. He makes a call to Langley and speaks to Guardian. Guardian agrees to house sit and watch Mrs. Baker and take care of any needs she may have until Travis gets back. Travis tells Mrs. Baker what is happening and waits for Guardian to arrive. Travis makes the introductions and heads out to the airport. It's time to take care of the Williamson situation once and for all. Travis has looked forward to this for months. He knows Williamson will still be on guard but is probably feeling better about the situation. Travis will use this to his advantage.

THIRTY-SEVEN

Casablanca, Morocco

Travis arrives at the airport in DC and books a flight under the alias Gordon Schumacher, an engineer from Topeka, Kansas. He'll take TWA to Nouasseur. He'll arrive at Terminal 2 and catch a taxi to Casablanca, 30km away. He's booked a room at Hotel Colbert, 3 Rue Chaoula, Casablanca.

Travis arrives at his hotel and checks in. He will rest today and start the search tomorrow. Travis settles into his room and places a call to Langley Op's Center. He gets Squeaker on the phone and tells him what he needs. Travis relaxes and runs scenarios through his mind as to where and how he'll take care of Williamson. It will be extremely slow and painful - not a quick job. Travis doses off with visions of mayhem in his mind.

Travis wakes up the next morning refreshed and ready to go. He calls Langley and talks to Squeaker and finds out that Williamson is staying at the Hotel Central, 20 Place Ahmad El Bid Aoui, Casablanca. His room is on the fourth floor. How does Travis know he is in Casablanca? He remembers when he was training these guys; Williamson obsessed with the movie Casablanca. He remembers him saying if he ever has the money, he would live in Casablanca.

Casablanca is like most Moroccan cities. Tightly packed buildings with narrow streets. Lots of squares and fountains and mosques.

Travis catches a cab to the Hotel Central to verify that Williamson is there and to start his recon of Williamson's habits and routines. He arrives and takes up his roost in the Plaza outside the hotel. He watches everyone coming and going out of the hotel. It doesn't take long for him to spot Williamson leaving the hotel. He follows him to a café. Travis isn't too worried that Williamson will spot him as he has let his hair and beard grow out. Williamson would have to get a very hard and close up view of Travis to recognize him. Travis will make sure that didn't happen until he was ready for it to happen. After Williamson eats, he heads out to the local marketplace and does some shopping. After he's done he ventures back to the hotel and stays there the rest of the day.

He follows this routine three days in a row. Travis is starting to put his plan together. Travis notices that Williamson is carrying a pistol with him at all times so this will have to be figured into the plan. Travis knows just how good he is with a weapon and with his hands. He helped train this monkey. But Travis knows he didn't teach him everything. Some things are reserved for a need to know basis, and he didn't need to know at the time.

On the fourth day, Williamson varied from his normal routine. After going to the marketplace, he went to the Mosque and spent three hours there. Travis had no idea what he was doing there. Travis followed Williamson and on the eighth day Williamson did the same routine as on the fourth day.

Travis went back to his hotel and tried to figure out what Williamson was doing at the Mosque every fourth day. Travis decided to go to the Mosque and see for himself what might be going on. Travis sits outside the Mosque and watches for anything out of the ordinary. He knows Williamson isn't there for the religion. Not a guy like Williamson. He has to be there for another reason. Most likely it has something to do with money.

Suddenly, Travis notices that men are bringing crates into the Mosque. It looks like military writing on the crates. Travis gets out his binoculars and takes a look. He can make out some of the words on the side of the crates. Just what Travis thought. Looks like Williamson is dealing in illegal arms. That would fit right in with Williamson, anything to make a buck. Travis heads back to his hotel and starts laying out his plan. He decides to take him at his hotel and use Williamson's own room to get things done. Travis knows how to keep him quiet while he goes about his work. Travis prepares his tools for the work coming up. He'll take Williamson tomorrow.

THIRTY-EIGHT

Hotel Central

Travis waits at the hotel for Williamson to return. He has stationed himself around the corner from the stairs. Travis has a needle filled with the appropriate dosage of succinylcholine to take him down but not kill him. He also has the equipment in his bag to keep him breathing. Travis will inject him, get the key out of his pocket, drag him in the room and then deal with him the way he wants. Travis hears him coming.

He waits for him to come around the corner and injects him. Williamson's eyes go wide as he realizes he can't move, and he goes down hard. Travis grabs him by the collar and gets the key to his room. He drags him in the room and starts taking care of his breathing. Once he has him stable, he moves him to the bed and gets him secured. Travis monitors his vitals to make sure everything's going well. Williamson is awake but cannot move. He'll be able to feel everything that Travis does to him, but he cannot make any noise. His throat is paralyzed along with the rest of his body. Travis inserts the breathing tubes needed to keep Williamson alive. He then tapes Williamson's head down. Travis does this for a specific reason.

"I'm going to ask you a series of questions. I want you to blink once for yes and twice for no. Do you understand?"

Williamson blinks once.

"Do you know who I am?"

Williamson blinks once.

"Do you know why I'm here?"

Williamson blinks once.

"Have you ever been deer hunting and skinned a deer?"

Williamson blinks once.

"Have you ever skinned a deer while it was still alive?"

Williamson blinks twice.

"It would hurt like a son of a bitch if you did it while they were still alive. It's a little trick I learned from the cartels in Columbia. And since you want to take their money for killing my family, I'm going to show you what it feels like to experience that."

Williamson blinks twice and closes his eyes. Travis sticks his finger in Williamson's eye to make him open them.

"First I'm going to cut your eyelids off, so you won't be able to close your eyes. I want you to see everything I do to you."

Williamson blinks twice.

"Sorry, but you don't have a choice in the matter this time. You see, your ass is mine now and I'm going to make this as painful as possible and make it last as long as your heart will hold out. You're mine now you son of a bitch!"

Williamson blinks twice several times in a row.

Travis pulls surgical clamps out of his bag and attaches them to Williamson's eyelids and lifts them up. He then takes a scalpel out and starts to cut the eyelids off. First the top and then the bottom ones.

"Damn, that's got to hurt like a bitch! It makes me hurt just looking at you."

Travis sees tears roll out of the corners of Williamson's eyes. "Don't cry yet. We're just getting started. We haven't even gotten to the good stuff yet. I thought you would be tougher than this."

Next, Travis starts cutting the skin around the outside of the soles of his feet. He cuts across the ball of the foot just below the toes. He then pries the skin up and starts peeling it back toward the heel of the foot.

"How does that feel so far? Are you comfortable? Of course, you're not. Right about now you're hoping that you'll pass out. But I know just when to stop to keep that from happening. Hell, that's just one foot. We still have one to go. But I'm going to rest for a minute and let the pain really start to take a hold of you. Don't go anywhere, I'll be right back."

Travis walks away and decides what he wants to do next. He spends a few minutes getting something to drink and cleaning up a little. Now he's ready to continue.

"Now I'm going to make an incision all the way around your leg just above the ankle and then up the outside and inside of your leg and then peel the skin back to your knee. Do you want to watch? Oh, that's right, you have to watch. Try not to pass out on me if you can." Travis sets about doing just what he described to Williamson. Just as he's finishing up, Williamson passes out from the pain.

Travis takes a break and waits for Williamson to wake up. Travis has all the time in the world to inflict pain on this man and inflict pain he will. He checks and sees it's time for the next injection in order to keep Williamson at the level he wants him awake and alive and feeling everything he does to him. Travis isn't some savage animal, but he does get a measure of peace from causing this man pain for what he did to his family. It's not what Travis was raised to do, but it's something Travis needs to do.

"Hey asshole. Wakey, wakey!! It's time for your next dose of pain. You actually lasted longer last time than I thought you would. This time will be shorter as the pain just keeps compounding itself in your system. It must feel like your legs and feet are on fire. Just wait until I do the same thing on the other leg. Damn, I would not want to be you right now. Stay awake and watch this." Travis repeats the same procedure on the other leg and Williamson passes out right as Travis starts peeling the skin back.

Travis takes a break and freshens up. This is going to take a long time to finish, unless Travis grows bored and decides to finish it early.

Travis has already gone into the night and he's getting tired. He decides to grab a couple of hours rest before continuing. He checks Williamson and gives him the necessary dosage to keep him at the level he needs long enough to grab some sleep.

Travis wakes in the early morning and checks on Williamson. He injects him again and makes ready to start. He gets things ready and begins where he left off. He moves to the upper thighs and then to the stomach and chest. By the time Travis accomplishes this, the sun's coming up. He decides to stop and clean up. After cleaning up, he decides to go get some coffee and breakfast. He injects Williamson who has passed out yet again.

Travis returns about an hour and a half later refreshed and ready to inflict more pain on his victim. He knows he should go ahead and end it, but he feels he needs to inflict more pain before he does.

"Wakey, wakey asshole. It won't be long now. I'm going to remove your fingerprints and take the skin off your face to make it hard to identify you when they find you. I want you to be thrown in an unmarked grave to rot with nobody knowing who you are."

Travis sets about doing just what he told Williamson he was going to do. First he removes the fingerprints by cutting the skin off of his fingertips. Then he makes an incision around his face and lips and eyes and slowly peels the skin off. No one will be able to identify him now. Travis steps back and looks at his handy work. He's satisfied and decides it's time to end it. Travis goes about wiping the room down for fingerprints and cleaning up. He walks over to Williamson.

"Well, as much as I have enjoyed this, parting is such sweet sorrow. Not really. I'm going to put you out of your misery now." Travis gives Williamson a massive dose of succinylcholine and watches as Williamson's heart stops beating. Travis is pleased to have kept his promise. He's not proud of what he did, but it was necessary to accomplish his ultimate goal. Travis turns and calmly walks out and heads to the airport and gets on the plane and comes home.

THIRTY-NINE

Washington DC

Travis arrives and goes through customs. He gets his car and heads home. On the ride home, his mind wonders back to what he did in Morocco. He knows there's a special place in Hell for him and he can live with that as long as he gets his revenge for Sarah and Jamie. Travis arrives at home and goes inside.

Travis is greeted by Guardian and Mrs. Baker who's gushing about how sweet Guardian has been while he was gone. Travis looks at Guardian, who's blushing and breaks out laughing.

"Well, I'm glad that he took such good care of you while I was gone. I knew he would."

"Oh, my goodness yes he did. He basically waited on me hand and foot."

"I take it everything went well and there were no problems."

"No, Skipper. Everything was ten by ten. She's really a fascinating lady. She has seen and done stuff most of us will never know."

"Why do you call him Skipper?"

"It's a military term and he is my boss and runs the team, so he is the Skipper. Like on a ship. He's in charge."

"Oh, I see."

All three laugh and Guardian pulls Travis to the side. "I'm glad you're home. The arraignment went as expected and the sentencing was handed down for Baker. He's to be executed Friday."

"I never thought I would say this, but why so soon?"

"He asked for the sentence to be carried out as soon as possible. He said he wanted to have it done so the media would leave his wife alone."

"Does she know about any of this yet? Has she talked to him?"

"She knows he's been sentenced, but she said she wanted you with her when she talks to him. He's been moved to federal prison at FCI Bennettsville."

"Ok. I'll call Turner, and have it set up for us to visit Baker. Guardian, thanks for taking good care of her while I was gone. I know it sounds weird, but I like keeping my promises, even if it's to the lowest scumbag on the face of the earth. Has she said anything about how she feels or what she might say to him?"

"No Skipper, not a word other than to say she wanted you there when she did talk to him. She said you make her feel safe."

"Thanks again."

Travis thinks about this as he goes to his bedroom and drops off his bags. He has a funny feeling about why Mrs. Baker wants him with her when she talks to Baker. It makes him feel good that she feels safe with him there, but something's making the hair on the back of his neck stand up and he can't quite put a finger on it yet. Travis goes back into the living room and says his goodbyes to Guardian as he's ready to leave.

"Thanks again for taking such good care of Mrs. Baker."

"No problem, Skipper. Talk to you soon."

"Now Mrs. Baker, let's have a chat, shall we?"

"Please call me Joanne."

"All right, Joanne. I understand that you know about your husband's sentencing?"

"Yes, Lewis told me about it."

"If I may ask, why do you want me with you when you talk to him?"

"Because right now, I'm scared of the man who used to be my husband. Right now, I don't know who he is, and I certainly don't know what he's capable of. I would feel much safer with you there. Now let's talk about your choice of school for the scholarships."

"All right, Joanne. I know Sarah's favorite school was Texas A&M. I think it would be appropriate to have scholarships there in her honor."

"Texas A&M it is then. I'll have my lawyer ……. I just realized that my lawyer is his lawyer. I was going to say I would have my lawyer set everything up, but I guess in light of everything that has happened, I need to find a new attorney. I'll do that tomorrow and get the ball rolling. Travis, I really can't thank you enough for all you've done for me."

"No need to thank me for anything. I want to thank you for the way you have chosen to honor my family."

Somewhere in the back of Travis's mind, something just didn't ring true or right about all of this. He had better figure it out quick before something bad happens. Travis decides to have the guys run rotating shifts and stand watch until he can figure this thing out. He calls Langley and talks to the team. Travis sets it up to have a barbecue the next afternoon at his place for the team. He hates having the guys run private security for him, but until he gets a handle on what's going on, it's probably best.

The guys show up for the barbecue and Travis lets them in on what he wants. He apologizes for not having their families this time but vows next time will be different. Travis has been smoking Boston butts all morning. He starts to pull them out of the smoker one at a time and has Lee start chopping. Thomas comes up to Travis and asks him why all the extra security. Travis and Thomas have been friends since middle school and joined the Marine Corps together. Travis tells him about the weird feeling he has that the other shoe hasn't dropped yet. Thomas knows how Travis's hunches go, and 99 percent of the time, they're right on the money. Thomas could count on one hand the number of times Travis has been wrong about a hunch. Thomas says he'll let the others know. He tells Travis to let them know when he figures it out.

There's something about Joanne that's just not sitting right with Travis. He still believes she doesn't know what her husband was doing, but at the same time, her reaction to this whole thing has been off just enough to make Travis worry. He'll put his finger on it sooner or later. He just hopes it's not too late before he does.

Travis starts to think about how Joanne has reacted to the various stages of her husband's career unraveling and the more he thinks about it, the more lack of concern and caring she has shown. He starts to think about how easily Baker had given up and pled guilty. He knew the kind of person Baker was and he had expected a Hell of a lot more fight about everything than he had gotten. Something is rotten in the henhouse for sure. Travis just needs to figure out what it is. Well, the food is done, and it's time for sharing and comradery with the team. He'll worry about this later.

Travis spends the next few hours enjoying the down time he has with the guys. As the day winds down and the food disappears, Travis and the men get ready for the first night of security detail. Most of the guys leave, except for the ones on duty tonight. Travis heads inside and goes to his room to relax. He decides to call Turner at home.

"Director Turner, this is Travis. I hate to bother you at home, but I think we need to talk."

"What's on your mind, Travis?"

Travis fills Turner in on the hunch he has about something being not quite right with this whole situation.

"It's funny you should say that. I've been doing some digging of my own and I've got some things I think you need to take a look at. Can you be in my office first thing in the morning?"

"I'll be there at eight sharp."

"Good. See you then." Travis hangs up and wonders what the director has found.

FORTY

Director Turner's Office

When Travis arrived at Turner's office, Turner was there waiting for him.

"Come on in, Travis."

"Thank you Director."

"I have some things I think you need to look at, Travis. I've been doing a little background on Mrs. Baker. Do you know what her maiden name is?"

"No Sir. What is her maiden name?"

"Rothschild."

"Not 'The Rothschild'?"

"The one and only."

"Holy shit, Sir."

"It appears from the records that she inherited $300,000,000 when her father died. She was the one who financed Baker's political career. Records show she spent about $30,000,000 getting him elected mayor of Napa, then governor of California, then his Senate seat. The funny part is, after he won the Senate seat, her money disappeared. I did some digging and found out she has $450,000,000 in offshore accounts."

"Well, that would certainly explain some things I was wondering about. So, she had the money and he was broke until he married her. How the Hell did he manage to land a Rothschild?"

"It looks more like a partnership than a marriage. She put up the money to get him elected with the understanding that once he got in the Senate, he would use his seat to gain power and money."

"Well, he certainly made good on his end. He has more power than anyone on Capitol Hill. What's bothering me so much is how easy he rolled over and pled guilty. With that much power and control, you would think he would fight until his dying breath to keep control. I'm not buying this crap about being concerned for his wife. Hell, a man like that would throw her under the bus in a heartbeat to keep his power and control. Hell, he would sell his own mother out to maintain his status. People like that don't change overnight. Something is hinky in Denmark."

"I agree 100 percent. But what the Hell could it be?"

"I don't know yet, but you can bet your bottom dollar I'm going to find out. Wait, you said she inherited $300,000,000 and has $450,000,000 in offshore accounts? Where in the Hell did the other $150,000,000 come from?"

"Maybe it came from his dealings with the cartels."

"Maybe, but what's bugging me now is the talk I had with her about finances. She said she had no idea how much they were worth. She said they never talked about finances. I just don't see a Rothschild handing over her money and not knowing what's going on with it."

"That's a good point."

"Whose name is the account in?"

"The account's in hers."

"Maybe she started the account to hide assets from the government for tax purposes and he took it over after he made the deal with the cartels. But why would she lie about not knowing about the finances? She's bound to be smart enough to know we would find out her maiden name and ask questions."

"That part really makes no sense at all."

"I can see the money coming from the cartel deals, but her not knowing about it is really throwing me off. I don't want to confront her until we figure this thing out."

"Yeah, confronting her now would only make her go further underground than she already is. I'll keep looking into this and keep you informed of what I find."

"Ok. I'll do some investigating myself and maybe between the two of us, we can figure out what in the Hell is going on. In the meantime, I need you to set up a visit for me and Mrs. Baker to see the Senator. She says she wants me to be there with her because she's afraid of him. Something about that's not sitting right with me either."

"Consider it done. I'll call with the details."

"Thank you, Sir. Let me know what you find and I'll do the same."

Travis leaves the director's office and heads down to the Op's Center to talk to the guys before going home.

FORTY-ONE

Travis's Home

Travis arrives at his home after his meeting and finds Joanne in the kitchen cooking. He goes to his room to do some thinking. This whole finance thing has him confused. Travis just can't believe that a Rothschild couldn't know about the money in the offshore account. He knew she had to be lying about that, and if she lied about that, what else was she lying to Travis about?

Joanne knocks on Travis's door. "Come in."

"I don't mean to bother you, but I was wondering if you liked Beef Wellington with Au Gratin Potatoes and a fresh salad? All homemade, of course."

"That sounds absolutely delicious."

"I hope you don't mind but I sent Lewis to the market with a list. I figured with your hospitality, the least I could do was make a nice dinner for you and the boys."

"I don't mind at all. They're here to help you when I'm not around. I really appreciate your going to all the trouble to fix that for us."

"It's not a problem at all. I love to cook for people that enjoy eating."

Travis laughs. "Well, you can bet that these boys like to eat. That's for sure. I'm sure they'll be very thankful to get a decent meal for a change."

"Do you drink wine, Travis?"

"Yes ma'am, I do."

"Would you care to join me for a glass before dinner?"

"I would really enjoy that. Shall we?"

Travis thought to himself, *maybe a little wine will put a new spin on this mess that makes sense.*

Travis joined Joanne in the kitchen for a glass of wine and conversation. "How long have you been cooking today, Joanne?"

"Oh, I started just after you left this morning and have been doing so ever since. You'll be pleased to know that I found a lawyer this morning and got the ball rolling on setting everything up for the scholarships. I told him to put the money in a trust fund for the next 20 years."

"Joanne, that's so gracious of you, but that's a lot of money. I don't want you to cut yourself short."

"Don't you worry about that now, Travis. You told me that my husband was worth over $40,000,000, did you not?"

"Yes ma'am, I did."

"Well, I certainly don't need that much money to live on, now do I?"

Travis thought about the $450,000,000 in the offshore account. "No, I guess you know what's best for you."

Travis stands there drinking his wine and for the first time, takes a really good look at Joanne while she goes about cooking. He realizes that she is a very attractive woman. She is about five foot four with sparkling green eyes and brown hair. She has a very nice figure. She cuts quite the figure as his dad would say. Travis laughs to himself as he thinks about his dad. He would have to visit his parents after all this was settled.

Joanne caught Travis's interested glance and it made her feel good to know that a man of Travis's age would look at her that way. She had always tried to keep herself in good shape and presentable, as her mother used to say. She felt like for a woman of 50 years old, she was doing something right. She might consider making a move later on down the line. Travis, after all, was a very handsome man and he definitely took good care of himself. You could probably wash clothes on his abdomen. After she got rid of her old man of a husband, why not treat herself to something special for a change?

Travis knew Joanne had seen him looking at her and smiled to himself. He had no sexual interest in her, but if she thought he did, maybe that could work in his interest. Travis raised his glass. "Here's to a long and happy friendship."

Joanne raised her glass and smiled. *Here's to more than friendship*, she thought to herself. Hell, she couldn't remember the last time her husband had looked at her that way, or for that matter, the last time he had touched her. He was too busy with his damn career for anything like that. "Here's to a long and happy friendship indeed."

"How long before dinner's ready, Joanne?"

"Should be ready in about an hour."

Travis excused himself to go let the boys know about the wonderful dinner Joanne was preparing for them. He told them it should be ready in about an hour and to come on then to get ready. He then went back in the kitchen. He noticed when he got back that Joanne had undone another couple of buttons on her top and was bending over in his direction a lot more. He found this very amusing. Hell, she was old enough to be his mother. Travis did like older women though. He could definitely enjoy her beauty and figure. He would play along for now.

"So, Travis, what amount of money per year would you like for the scholarships to be?"

"I'm leaving that entirely up to you. I'm just grateful that you're willing to do this for my family."

"How does $20,000 a year for each of the two scholarships sound?"

"That sounds like a lot of money. That's $40,000 a year for 20 years - almost a $1,000,000."

"That's $800,000 to be exact, and you let me worry about that. It's the least I can do considering what my husband has done to you and your family. I think I can live very comfortably on $39,000,000 plus dollars."

"So, have you thought about what you're going to do after all this is said and done?"

"I've given some thought about becoming a philanthropist and spending my money on worthy causes. How does that sound to you?"

"Sounds like a very noble cause to me. Maybe do something with the arts or the underprivileged."

"That sounds truly noble indeed. Perhaps choose the underprivileged. I was also thinking about children's cancer research. The arts already have so many patrons."

"Sounds perfect to me. By the way, you look lovely this evening." Travis thought to himself, *I can play the game for a while and see what I can get out of you, information wise. If I play this right, you might just give up the game with a little pillow talk.*

"Why, thank you kind Sir. It's been a while since anyone has said that to me." Joanne thought to herself, *if he keeps this up, I may speed up the timetable and move a lot sooner. I could live with being a sugar mama for a while. Hell, I've been a sugar mama for my entire marriage. At least he's young and good-looking.* Joanne smiled to herself.

The phone rang and Travis excused himself it. "Hello?"

"Travis, this is Director Turner."

"Yes, Sir. What can I do for you?"

"I have it arranged for you and Mrs. Baker to visit the Senator day after tomorrow at three o'clock. You can visit for about an hour. I had them waive the usual security searches so she wouldn't be uncomfortable."

"Thank you, Sir. I'll let her know. I may do a little security check myself before we leave. I still don't trust her yet."

"That might be a good idea, Travis. I don't see how she could do anything with you there, but you never know."

"My thoughts exactly, Sir."

Travis hung up the phone and started thinking about how he might go about searching her before they left. He could play this a couple of different ways. He could try to become involved with her so he could watch her dress. He could explain that it was part of the routine before a visit. Better he do the search than some stranger at the prison. Or he could explain that when they get there, she'll have to be searched. He would think about it and see how things went tonight. Just as Travis walked back in the kitchen, he saw that Joanne looked a little wobbly. He went around the counter just as she seemed to swoon. Travis grabbed her around the waist and held her up. He helped her to a chair.

" Are you all right?"

"I don't know what happened. It must be a combination of the wine and the heat. I'm so sorry if I scared you."

"You didn't scare me. I was just worried you might fall and hurt yourself. I hope I didn't grab you too hard."

"Oh, no. I'm just glad you were there. You have a very strong grip."

"You sure I didn't hurt you?"

"No, you didn't. Thank you for catching me. I just need a minute to catch my breath and cool down. It's been a long time since I had a young man grab me around my waist."

"And a very nice waist it is."

"You keep that up and you'll make me blush."

"I bet you're beautiful when you do blush."

"Why, thank you. Do you think I'm beautiful?"

"Very. You're a spectacular looking woman who obviously takes very good care of herself. Now you're blushing, and you're beautiful when you do."

"You keep that up and I might just have to take advantage of you later." Joanne laughs nervously.

Travis laughs and leans down and kisses her on the forehead. "You keep that up and I might just let you."

Joanne reaches out and hugs Travis around the waist. She could feel his muscular young body pressed against her. She must have had more wine than she thought. She held her breath to see if he would return the hug.

Travis reaches down and hugs her back. "You better be careful, or I might take advantage of you."

"You keep that up and I might just let you."

They both laugh. About that time, they hear the guys coming in and they step apart.

"Hey Travis, Mrs. Baker. Everything ok?"
"Yeah, she got a little overheated cooking and I had her sit down for a minute."

"Are we too early?"

"No, everything's ready. I just need to get it on the table. You boys get washed up."

Travis and Joanne went about getting everything on the table and ready for dinner. The guys came back in and they all sit down to enjoy the wonderful meal Joanne had prepared.

"So, guys, if you don't mind me asking, how do you all know each other?"

"Skipper, I mean Travis and I have known each other since middle school. We grew up together and joined the Marines together. We got separated after boot camp and we both got recruited for Force Recon School. When we graduated, Travis went off to Sniper School. When he graduated, with honors I might add, The Marines gave him the opportunity to form his own team and I was the first one chosen. After that, he handpicked each of the guys on the team for special skills they brought to the team. We've been together ever since. We ran 300 missions together. We were a 15 man team and we lost three members on active duty. Now we operate as a 12 man team."

"That's very impressive. And what sort of skills do each of you have?"

"I'm the sniper and what they call overwatch. I watch over the guys and take out any threats that come our way to make sure the guys are safe. I run the team."

"I'm the climbing and rappelling specialist."

"I'm the explosives expert."

"I'm the water expert."

"Lee is the Ariel expert."

"Stan is the communications expert."

"Lewis is the public liaison."

"Robert is the blockade specialist."

"William is the diversion specialist."

"Wilson is the team's muscle."

"Terry is the resident wizard."

"Leon is the security specialist."

"I see what you mean when you say everyone on the team brings something special with them. It must be very exciting and dangerous."

"It can be both. Usually more dangerous than exciting. Everything we do is classified."

"What do you mean when you say classified?"

"It's all top secret and cannot be talked about."

"Oh, I see. Like top secret in the movies?"

They all laugh, and Travis says "Yeah, something like that."

Travis and Joanne are the only ones drinking wine with dinner. The guys are all drinking sweet tea. Everyone finishes dinner and the guys go back on duty. Travis tells Joanne to sit at the counter and he will clean the dishes since she was gracious enough to make dinner. Neither speaks of what happened earlier. There's no tension in the room. They're both relaxed from the wine. Travis finishes the dishes, says good night to Joanne, and goes to his room.

Travis gets ready for bed and closes his eyes. He prays to Sarah and Jamie for forgiveness for things he has done and might have to do to bring a conclusion to this ordeal. Travis lays down and is going over the events of the day when he hears a soft knock on his door.

"Come in."

"I don't mean to bother you, Travis."

"It's ok, Joanne. What can I do for you?"

"I was wondering if you might not mind holding me for just a bit. With everything that happened earlier, it just felt so nice to have someone hold me. It's been so long since that happened. I know that your wife is still fresh in your mind, and I'll understand if you say no."

"Come in. I must admit it felt nice for me too."

Joanne comes into the room and slips into bed beside Travis. Travis puts his arm around her, and she snuggles into his warm and hard body. They lay like this for a while and Travis notices that Joanne has dozed off. He smiles and dozes off himself. Travis wakes sometime during the night as he feels Joanne leaving the bed. He doesn't let her know he's awake. Travis rises early the next morning and heads to Langley.

FORTY-TWO

Langley Op's Center

Travis arrives at the Op's Center bright and early. He starts going through the intel that Turner gave him on Joanne's background. What he can't figure out is her not knowing, or should he say, acting like she knows nothing about the money. He put a trace on the offshore account to see if any new transactions have happened. Travis still can't figure out why Baker rolled over so easy. Travis goes over and over the information and suddenly it hits him like a ton of bricks! Travis receives a hit on the account. Joanne has withdrawn $1,000,000 - enough to cover the cost of the scholarships. This just confirms his suspicions. Travis needs to see Turner immediately. He goes upstairs to Turner's office.

"Come in, Travis. What can I do for you?"

"I've figured it out. Baker's nothing more than a puppet in this whole thing. That's why he rolled over so easy. I put a trace on the offshore account, and I got a hit just now. A $1,000,000 withdrawal. Baker's in Federal Prison; he has no access to the account. It has to be Joanne. That's the amount she needs to do the scholarships in Sarah and Jamie's names. Rather than pull it from the account under her husband's name, she pulled it out of the offshore account."

"So how does that make Baker a puppet in all this?"

"Don't you see? Joanne's the one behind all this. She's the one running the show and used him as a puppet to orchestrate this whole thing. That's why he rolled over - to protect her identity."

"I'm still not putting all the pieces together. Break it down for me."

"Joanne told me she knew nothing about the finances of her husband. I tested her again last night and got the same response. If she knew nothing about the finances, she wouldn't know about the offshore account. By making the withdrawal today, she showed that she knows about it. Therefore, she knows about all the rest, because she's the mastermind behind it all. She's the one responsible for the deals Baker did on Capitol Hill and with the cartels. Hell, she probably made the deals and used him as a failsafe in case anything happened. That way, he takes the fall and she walks away scot-free to continue working with the cartels."

"Your logic makes sense, but we need hard facts to prove any of this. Do you have any of that, other than the withdrawal and her telling you she knew nothing about the finances?"

"Not yet, but I have an idea how I might get some. It will involve me getting to know her a lot better and more personally, a fact I'm not fond of, but it may be the only way to get to her. I laid some groundwork last night just in case something like this might occur. I'll give you more details later."

"What if you're wrong about all this?"

"Then the worst that will happen is I embarrass myself and have to apologize. If I'm right, her ass is going down one way or the other. I'm telling you now, if she tries to run, I'll drop her where I find her. This can end your way or my way; she will decide which happens. I hope for her sake it happens your way. My way will be slow and painful."

"I hope for her sake she chooses the right way. I received word about the body found in the Hotel Central in Morocco. Remind me never to get on your bad side, Travis."

"I'll fill you in as data becomes available."

"Be careful Travis. If you're right, and I think you are, this lady is no amateur. She has a plan and a backup plan and a backup plan for that backup plan. Just watch your back. I don't want to get word there's a knife in it."

"You know me, all in."

FORTY-THREE

Travis's Home

Travis arrives home and finds Joanne in the kitchen again. Travis opens a bottle of Cabernet Sauvignon and pours two glasses. He walks up behind Joanne, sets the glasses down, wraps his arms around her waist and kisses her neck. She jumps, turns around, and kisses Travis on the lips, full and passionate. Travis returns the passion.

"Why did you leave last night?"

"I woke up and felt foolish being there. You're young enough to be my son."

"I'm also old enough to be your lover if you want me to be."

"I do admit it felt wonderful to have your arms wrapped around me like that. Why would you want an old lady like me?"

"You're beautiful and vibrant. Why would any man refuse to have you?"

"I'm just used to not being taken care of in that way for so long, that I just started doubting myself as a woman."

"If the flesh is willing, let the mind follow and have what you need and want. You deserve to treat yourself with respect and have those feelings returned by someone willing and able to do just that."

"Are you willing? Do you find me attractive and am I good enough for you?"

"I find you very beautiful and you're definitely good enough for any man in his right mind. Let's have some wine and see where things go from there."

Travis grabs the wine glasses and heads for the living room and sets them down by the fireplace. He builds a fire and settles in beside Joanne on the floor. Joanne has brought the bottle with her. They settle in next to each other and enjoy the fire, the wine and each other's company. Travis silently asks for Sarah and Jamie's forgiveness for things he knows are about to happen. Joanne silently thinks to herself, *I have finally found a man like I deserve instead of an old man with no feelings.*

Travis slowly eases Joanne backwards and moves next to her. He leans down and tenderly but passionately kisses her. Joanne reaches up and wraps her arms around Travis's neck and returns the kiss with the same passion. Travis stands and helps Joanne up. He takes her hand and leads her to his bedroom. He excuses himself for a moment and as he is retrieving the wine glasses and bottle, pauses in the kitchen to grab an extra bottle. Travis thinks to himself, *I may need to get loaded for this.* He returns to the room and closes the door. He slowly undresses

Joanne, picks her up, and places her on the bed. They spend the afternoon exploring each other and making love. As day turns to evening, they lay back in each other's arms.

Travis is startled by the sudden sound of small arms gun fire. He recognizes the sound of an AK-47. Travis tells Joanne to get in the closet and close the door. He throws on some clothes, grabs his go bag by the door, and races outside to see what's going on. He sees muzzle flashes by the back wall and looks around to locate his men. He then looks to see where the incoming gunfire is coming from. The muzzle flashes are coming from the back wall.

Travis pulls his 1911 45 from his go bag and his M16aA1 from his bag and starts to circle around towards the back wall. He gets to Thomas and motions for him to go right and hold. He signals Lewis to head for the back wall. Travis slowly starts making his way toward the back wall on the left side. Travis reaches the back wall and peeks over. He sees four men in a boat trying to tie up to the dock. He stands and fires at the one on the dock trying to grab the rope. He goes down and Travis tracks to the boat and fires twice. Two more go down. That leaves one in the boat. The last man swings around and fires at Travis. The waves cause his shot to go wide and Travis pumps one more round downrange and the last man goes down. Travis signals the others all clear and they converge at the back gate. They slowly make their way out onto the dock. They check the bodies and find no identification on any of them. Travis can tell they're Columbian. The cartel sent a hit squad. It was just pure luck that Travis had the boys here standing guard. "Looks like I'm still popular with the cartel. You guys clean this up and I'll check on Joanne and call Turner."

"Roger that, Skipper."

Travis goes back to the house and tells Joanne what has happened. He tells her to go to her room and shut the door and don't come out unless he or one of the guys comes to get her.

Travis calls Turner. "Hello. Director, this is Travis. A cartel hit squad just showed up at my house."

"Are you and the guys ok?"

"Yeah, we're good. Managed to take them all out before they could get the boat docked and get on land."

"They came by the river?"

"Yes Sir, and there's only one person that could have told them where I was. Baker's in prison in isolation. He has no outside contact with anyone. That only leaves one person. I haven't even told you where my new house is. No one at the CIA has that information. I think we have confirmation of who the mastermind is in all this. She wants me eliminated before I can figure out she is really in control and not Baker."

"Sounds like you may be right about that. We still need proof to be able to bring her down."

"I know. I'm working on that. I'll see what intel I can gather from these guys, but I need you to send a clean-up team to my house. I have the boys starting the job already."

"Ok. Tell me the address and I'll have them there in 30 minutes."

Travis gives his address to Turner and goes out and tells the boys the clean-up team's on the way.

"If any neighbors show up, tell them we were setting off firecrackers and apologize for disturbing them."

"Roger, Skipper."

"Get the bodies inside the wall quickly in case someone shows up."

Travis's house doesn't have a second story, but one of the reasons Travis liked this house is that it has a tower in the center. The man who built the house was an avid bird watcher and built a tower with windows all the way around so he could sit up there and bird watch the river and woods. You can bet from now on Travis will have one of the boys or himself up there all the time until this is finished. Travis heads back to the house to get Joanne and see what story she plays about all this.

"Joanne, it's Travis. Open the door please."

Joanne opens the door and Travis goes inside.

"Are you all right?'

"Yeah, I'm good."

"Are the guys all right?"

"Yeah, they're all good."

"Thank God. I was so scared when I heard the shooting start. You sure you're ok? You're not wounded, are you? Come here and let me check."

"That's ok. I'm ok. How did you know it was gunfire and not firecrackers or something like that?"

"William used to shoot skeet in the backyard. I'm used to hearing gunshots."

"Oh, ok. I was just curious. Most women are not used to gunshots. I guess you had better stay in here tonight. There'll be some people here to clean up the mess out back and we don't want to raise any suspicions."

"That would probably be wise, although I would love to sleep in your arms tonight."

"I'd like that also, but we have to be careful."

"I understand. I guess I'll kiss you goodnight now, then."

Travis kisses Joanne goodnight and turns and walks out.

FORTY-FOUR

FCI Bennettsville

Travis gets up and prepares breakfast. Joanne joins him in the kitchen.

"Are you ready for your big day today?"

"I'm nervous."

"What are you nervous about?"

"Seeing him. Knowing it'll be the last time I see him. He may be a son-of-a bitch, but I was married to him for 30 years."

"That's understandable. Have you figured out what you're going to say to him?"

"I have no idea. What do you say to someone who's about to be executed?"

"I know what I'm going to say. I'm going to tell him there's a special place in Hell for someone like him. I'll see him when I get there, and I'll be sure he suffers for eternity when I do!"

"I don't think that would be appropriate for me to say, even if that's what I'm thinking."

"I guess it wouldn't be at that. I guess just tell him how you feel at the moment."

"I guess we need to be ready to leave about one o'clock. They have a strict rule about visitors being searched before they are allowed to visit a prisoner. I had them grant me a special disposition. They will be satisfied if I tell them I searched you personally. I won't search you, but I guess we need to dress in the same room so I can assure them that you have been searched and not be lying to them."

"I understand, and dressing with you in the room will not be a problem. Actually, I like the idea. It may help to relax me before we leave."

"I'm glad you understand."

Travis goes about his normal routine and gathers Joanne and prepares to leave. They drive out to Bennettsville and prepare to go in to see Baker.

"Travis Bones and Mrs. William Baker to see the Senator."

"Yes, Sir. We've been expecting you. It has been pre-approved for you to see him."

Travis and Joanne are taken back to see Baker. He looks drawn and has lost weight. He looks fragile and he doesn't look up as they come in.

Without looking up, Baker speaks to Joanne.

"I'm sorry for everything I have put you through. I never meant for any of this to happen."

"William, I'm not going to lie. I'm ashamed of you and everything you've put this man and his family through. I'm ashamed of everything you've done to this country."

Baker slowly looks up. Travis cannot believe the show that Joanne is putting on. He sees the look in Baker's eyes and knows that everything he suspects is true. Travis doesn't say anything yet. He's waiting to see what Baker has to say to Joanne. Travis sees the fire flash through Baker's eyes. Baker quickly looks down and hopes that Joanne nor Travis saw it. Joanne didn't notice.

"You know I'll be there when they hang your ass! I'll make sure that you pay and pay dearly for what you've done. I'll also make sure that anyone else involved pays also."

Joanne and Baker look at Travis simultaneously. Travis knows he has hit a nerve with these two. Baker smiles and Joanne looks like she's been slapped. It slowly dawns on Joanne that Travis may be smarter than she thought. She'll have to pry just a little tonight to try and find out what Travis thinks. If Travis has figured it out, Joanne's not sure what she'll do. She knows that Travis will stop at nothing to make sure that everyone involved in this will be punished. She'll have to put on her best face and try to pry information out of Travis with a little push from her womanly wiles. She's almost scared to push Travis to find out what he knows, but she has to. Baker has an expression on his face like the cat that ate the canary. Travis believes Baker is actually enjoying this.

"I'll be here tomorrow when they hang you. I'll enjoy it and I'll have my revenge when it happens."

"I will not be here when it happens tomorrow. Regardless of what you've done, I cannot be a witness to that."

Travis and Joanne leave Baker sitting there and head home. Baker can feel his mind slowly start to slip and slowly starts laughing. Low at first, then building into almost hysterical laughter as he is lead back to his cell.

FORTY-FIVE

Travis' Home

Travis and Joanne ride home in silence. Joanne's mind is racing a 1,000 miles an hour. Does Travis have any idea she's behind all this or is he just blowing hard to scare her husband? Travis is trying to figure out what he's going to do with Joanne. He can't decide if he wants to bring her to justice or if he wants justice served his way. It'll depend on how Joanne reacts and what she does. They arrive home and neither one feels like cooking, so they decide to order a pizza and have it delivered. They eat in silence. Finally, Joanne speaks.

"I need to do some shopping tomorrow. I need to get some clothes and some other things. Do you think it'll be ok if I go shopping while you're gone tomorrow?"

"I don't see why not. I can have one of the guys go with you for safety's sake."

"That won't be necessary. I can just run out quickly and come back. No need to bore the guys with my shopping for girly stuff."

"I guess that would be ok. I would just feel better if you had someone with you in case the media gets wind of anything."

"I won't be gone that long. I'll make it short and sweet. We can use this as a test to see if the media even knows where I am."

Travis is immediately suspicious of her intentions. He has a sneaky feeling that she's planning something. He'll have one of the boys shadow her and see what she's up to. Travis excuses himself and goes to his room to make some calls. He calls Langley and speaks with Squeaker. He tells Squeaker to monitor all calls from the house and let him know if anything suspicious comes up.

Travis lies down and starts trying to put together what Joanne's trying to do. He believes she may be trying to run on him but isn't sure how she might go about doing this without outside contact. He will call Squeaker in the morning and see if any calls were made. Travis dozes off. He wakes up in the morning and calls Langley. Squeaker tells him that a call was made just after midnight to a charter airline service at Washington Dulles International Airport. Looks like Travis may miss the hanging today after all.

Travis gets up and gets ready to go. He grabs his go bag and heads out the door before Joanne gets up and about.

Joanne gets up and finds that Travis has left already. She gets ready and leaves.

FORTY-SIX

Washington Dulles International Airport

Joanne Baker heads toward Dulles Airport. She drives around for half an hour trying to make sure no one is following her. She pulls into parking at Dulles and makes her way to the charter terminal. She shall not risk being seen with any baggage so she decided to go without any baggage and would buy all new things when she reaches her destination.

"Hello, I'm Joanne Baker. I have a chartered flight leaving at ten thirty for Medellin, Columbia."

"Yes, Mrs. Baker. We have your reservation. Do you have any baggage?"

"No. It's just me. No baggage. How long before the plane is ready?"

"The plane is fueled and waiting on you to board. It will be just a few minutes and we'll be ready."

"Thank you. I need to board as soon as possible."

Joanne sits down and nervously waits. She's thinking about how long she'll need to stay in

Columbia before she comes back to the U.S. under the passport in her maiden name.

"I guess Travis isn't as smart as I was giving him credit for. Just a few minutes and I'll be out of here and free. Travis can't touch me once I leave the U.S." Joanne is pulled out of her reverie.

"Mrs. Baker, you're free to board now. Have a nice flight."

"Thank you, I will."

Joanne boards the Grumman Gulfstream II. She goes to her seat and sits down. The pilot comes out of the cockpit and Joanne's blood runs cold.

"Hello, Joanne. Taking a trip, are we?"

"Travis! How in the Hell did you know about my flight?"

"I'm paid to know things like this."

"I thought you were going to watch my husband get hanged?"

"I couldn't pass up the opportunity to say goodbye, now could I, Joanne."

"How could you have possibly known what I was planning today?"

"What you don't seem to realize is that I'm not some hick from North Carolina that you can sleep your way around. I'm highly trained. I get paid to figure shit like this out. I know all about you."

"I don't know what you think you know, but you don't know anything about me."

"Let's get comfortable and I'll tell you a little story. You're Joanne Lynn Rothschild. Born into the Rothschild fortune. Even as a little girl you had ambitions of becoming more powerful than your grandfather. You ran all kinds of scams when you were in school. Even in high school, you had to have the most power and influence and when you didn't get your way, you would pay people to destroy anyone who opposed you. You met William Baker at a function thrown by your grandparents. He was older than you by 15 years. You really didn't care much for him, but you saw him as a way to get out from under your parent's and grandparent's rule. You wouldn't get your inheritance until you were married. You made everyone believe that you were madly in love with him, so you got married. You agreed to finance his political aspirations in return for doing whatever you told him to do. Even at 20 you had to be in control. Let's have a drink while I finish my story."

Travis gets up and pours himself and Joanne a glass of wine. As Joanne takes the glass, he sees her hands are shaking.

"Let's see, where was I, oh yeah, age 20. You put up the money and got your husband elected as mayor of Napa. That didn't give you enough power, so you had him run for governor of California. You had some powerful opposition to that, so you paid someone to create a scandal and forced the opposition to resign from the race. Almost immediately, you started priming him for bigger and better things. As you were doing this, you set into motion things that would give him power and influence. You started making sure that he found whatever dirt he could find on anyone around him and started doing favors so that they owed him, or should I say you, favors later on when he needed them. How am I doing so far?"

"You don't have any idea what I sacrificed to get him where he is today."

"You didn't sacrifice anything. You made sure of that. You don't do anything unless it benefits you. You then made him run for the Senate and you spent enough money and called in enough favors to make sure he won. That's when the real fun and power began. You met Escobar at a function you and your husband attended in Columbia. You immediately had the idea to get involved in the drug trade. Why not? You could make stupid money and the power itself was intoxicating to you. William didn't think it was a good idea, so you threatened to pull your power and support if he didn't go along with what you wanted. Any of this sounding familiar?"

"What's wrong with wanting power and prestige?"

"Nothing when it's done for the right reasons. But your reasons are anything but right. You forced William to get anything he could find on people so you could control elections and get who you wanted elected. That alone breaks multiple laws. You wanted to make sure none of your plans came under scrutiny. You wanted to be able to do whatever you wanted and to Hell with everyone else."

"How long have you known all this?"

"Some of it, a while, some of it you just confirmed for me. You see, background is easy to find out. What takes time is figuring out why someone does what they do and how they go about it. That's what I'm paid to do with people like you."

"What do you mean, people like me?"

"People who want to break the law and screw the good people of the United States of America."

"Don't give me that patriotic bullshit. If you had the chance, you would do the same things I've done."

"That's where you're wrong, my dear. Some people have a concise notion of what's right and what's wrong. Some of us refuse to step over that line."

"With all the killing you've done, you want to preach to me about right and wrong? You're just as guilty as I am."

"I kill for the good of my country. I take out people like you who want to harm the welfare of this country for the sake of power and money. I'll answer for what I've done, and I can live with that. You, on the other hand, don't think you've done anything wrong."

"So, what happens now? You don't honestly think I'm just going to give up and go to prison, do you?"

"No, I don't. I have something altogether different in mind for you. You're going to be an example to the cartel in Columbia."

"What do you mean, an example?"

"Have you ever heard the term Columbian Necktie?"

"No. What does that mean?"

"This!"

Travis lunges forward and slices Joanne's throat. He then proceeds to pull her tongue out through the wound.

"That's what I mean by Columbian Necktie!"

Travis pins a note to her and moves her to the seat facing away from the cockpit. Travis then steps back to the lavatory in the rear of the plane and washes up. He's very careful not to get blood on his clothes. That would never do. He has another appointment. Travis steps off the plane and tells the pilots that Mrs. Baker had a restless night and will be taking a nap. She has asked not to be disturbed until she reaches Columbia. Travis turns and walks away.

FORTY-SEVEN

FCI Bennettsville

Travis makes it to Bennettsville with 20 minutes to spare before the execution. The execution is set for twelve o'clock sharp. Travis makes his way into the room where Baker is to be hanged. The officials have not brought Baker in yet. Travis is relieved that he made it here in time. He wants to watch the expression on his face when he leans in close and tells him about Joanne's early departure, and about how she was going to leave him holding the bag for everything until he figured it out. Any bets the old bastard will have a smile on his face when they place the bag over his head?

The officials bring Baker into the room, and Travis asks for a few minutes to talk to him privately. They grant Travis his wish. Everyone leaves the room except Baker, who's in cuffs, and Travis.

"How are you feeling today, Bill?"

"How the Hell do you think I'm feeling! I'm about to be hanged because of your sorry ass!"

"That's good to know. I have five minutes with your worthless ass, and I intend to make the most of it." Travis moves in close to Baker so he won't be overheard by anyone. "Your precious little wife is on board a private jet bound for Columbia as we speak."

"That's good. Why's she going to Columbia?"

"Why don't you tell me why she would go to Columbia.

"I'm sure I wouldn't have any idea."

"You just can't tell the truth about your dear little wife, even though you're about to die because of her, can you?"

"What are you talking about?"

"I figured it out, you stupid son of a bitch! I know your wife is the true mastermind in all of this. You're not smart enough to plan everything that has happened."

Baker's eyes go wide at the thought that Travis may have figured everything out. He wonders why Travis let her get away if he figured it out.

"You're not smart enough to figure anything out. If you figured it out, as you say, Joanne would never have been allowed to leave like you say she did."

Travis leans in so close that his mouth is almost touching Baker's ear. "I didn't say that she was alive when the jet took off."

Baker steps away from Travis and his expression, in Travis's mind, is priceless. "What have you done to my wife?"

"Let's just say that, when the jet lands in Columbia, somebody's in for a BIG surprise. You see, I intercepted her when she boarded, and I had a little conversation with her before she took off."

"What kind of conversation?"

"We had, what I like to call, story time. She too, thought I wasn't smart enough to put it all together. She was wrong. I simply told her the facts that I had come to realize, and she was quite impressed. I told her about her past and how she financed your entire political career. I told her about how she pushed you to gain power and influence on Capitol Hill. I told her about the offshore account and how much money was in it and how the figures didn't add up to what was left of her inheritance. She became quite belligerent at this point."

"How did you manage to find out about the offshore account?"

"I do work for the CIA. There's not much we can't learn or get to if we really want to. You see, that's what really cleared things up for me. The money always tells the story. By the way, myself and the CIA thank you for the generous contribution that you and your wife are about to make to the agency."

"We're not making any such contribution!"

"Don't you see? That's the beauty in all this. The money in that account will be transferred to an account at the CIA. You have no family to claim the money, and no one but you and the CIA know about the account. Well, except the cartel, and I don't think, in retrospect, they'll be coming after the money. So you see, you have no say in the matter. You just lost your wife, career, $450,000,000 dollars and you're about to lose your life. All in all, a really good day at the office, I would say!"

"You cocky little son of a bitch! I'll see you rot in Hell for this!"

"And just how do you propose to do that, Bill? Your ass is about to swing from the end of a rope. Your bravado does you no good now. Have a good rest of your life. All two minutes of it."

Travis steps back from Baker just as the others come back into the room. They place a gag in Baker's mouth and place the hood over his head. Travis asks if he can be the one to put the noose around Baker's neck. They let Travis have the honor. They know what he's given up to earn that right.

All but the hangman step off the gallows and wait for the charges to be read aloud. The clock strikes twelve and the hangman pulls the lever. You can hear as Baker's neck snaps with a loud crack. Travis turns and walks out of the room with a smile on his face.

FORTY-EIGHT

Travis's Home

"This is Cory Stevens with NBC News with a breaking report out of Medellin, Columbia. The wife of disgraced Senator William Baker was found murdered on board a private jet when it landed in Columbia this evening. One can only speculate as to the reason for this tragedy. It's said that she had a note attached to her body that read:

"To whom it may concern: It's time to end this. This will be the result for anyone you see fit to send after this. There's no one, nor anyplace I cannot reach. For the good of your people, end this now."

"That's a mighty cryptic note if I may say so. What can this note possibly mean, and to whom was it intended? Hopefully someone can make sense of it and let us know more about it. We'll keep you informed of any updates to this story. This is Cory Stevens reporting. Now back to your regular programming."

Travis sits back and reflects upon what he has just watched, and he can only hope that the cartel takes his note seriously. Travis decides to call his mom.

"Hello, Mom? This is Travis."

"Travis honey, how are you doing? Is everything ok?"

"Yeah, everything's ok. I was just thinking about you and Dad and decided I'd call and see how y'all are doing."

"We're doing fine, honey. When are you going to come see us?"

"That's actually why I'm calling. I thought I might come and see y'all, if that's all right?"

"Of course it's all right. You can come see us anytime you want to. You know that."

"I know Mom, but I still like to check first. I'll come down in the morning. Can you and Dad pick me up at the airport? I'll call when I get in."

"Of course we can. You just call and let us know when. I love you."

"Love you too, Mom. See you tomorrow."

Travis sits back and thinks about his mom and dad. His mom is a little whisper of a thing. She stands at four feet nine inches tall. She always argues that she is five feet. Dad always kids her about that, saying that if you mash her hair down to the top of her head, she's only four feet nine. Travis laughs as he thinks about this. This is a sore subject with his mom. His dad stands six feet and is a true southern gentleman. He speaks softly and carries a very big stick, as Travis remembers anyway. He's worked hard all his life and taught these things to Travis. His mom is a stay-at-home mom who raised four kids.

Travis is the baby of the family and sooner than later realized that he could get by with nothing, as his mom had already been through it with the others first. Hell, his mom had a better spy network than the FBI. She never had to call anyone; they called her if they thought Travis was trying anything. Travis really laughed at this thought.

Travis calls Director Turner to make sure he can use the company jet for the visit. Director Turner assures him that's fine. He tells Travis to take as much time as he needs. He's definitely earned it. Travis calls and reserves the jet for first thing in the morning.

Travis meets the jet at eight o'clock and boards and tells the pilot to head for North Carolina - Raleigh to be exact.

The jet takes off and Travis settles in for the flight and starts thinking about home. This will be a short flight from DC to North Carolina. Travis thinks back to being in high school and his buddies. He remembers all the times he and the boys would cruise up and down main street on Saturday night. He remembers all the times they got in trouble for uncapping the headers on their cars and making way too much noise. The police would stop them and warn them to fix the problem before someone got arrested. He thinks about the girls he dated in high school. He seems to always date the cheerleaders. He smiles thinking about this. He wonders how much the town has changed. He hasn't been home since he got out of Basic in the Marines. Last time he came home, he and Sarah had just gotten married. He remembers his dad and mom coming to get them. His mom would not let them get into the car until Travis showed her the marriage license. Travis laughs about that. His mom and dad were very strict about letting any girl stay at their house that was not family. The same was true for his brother also. His brother had served in the Army twice. Travis didn't hold this against him though. Travis laughs remembering the times he rode his brother about the Army after he had graduated boot camp. He was looking forward to seeing his brother.

The pilot announced the approach to Raleigh. Travis fastened his seat belt and looked out the window just in time to see the large lake stretched out beneath him. He had grown up on that lake and it held some fond memories for him. The jet touched down and Travis disembarked and went inside to phone his parents. The airport seemed even smaller than he remembers. He guessed that was because of the bigger airports he was now accustomed to.

FORTY-NINE

Raleigh, North Carolina

Travis walked over to the pay phone and called his parent's home. They said they would be there in about an hour and a half. Travis hung up and walked outside to look around. He had never spent much time at the airport when he lived here. He remembered about the only time he came out here was with his friend Charles who had a Camaro that was suped-up and ran on jet fuel. Travis smiled when he thought about that car. Damn it was fast!

Travis wandered around until it was time for his parents to get there. He walked back over to the terminal and waited. His parents arrived and Travis scooped his mom up in his arms and gave her a big old bear hug. He sat her down and walked over to his dad and gave him a big hug too. Travis loved his parents and was glad to be home again.

The ride home was filled with his mom asking a hundred questions and Travis not having time to answer one before another came along. He laughed to himself about that.

"Are you home on leave?"

"No Mom, I'm not in the Marine Corps anymore. I left the Corps and went to work for the government."

"Which part of the government are you working for?"

"You know I can't tell you that. Let's just say that I'm still working for the good guys. Everything I do for them is classified just like in the Marines."

"So I still won't know where you are or what you're doing?"

"That's correct. It's not that I don't want you to know, I just can't tell you. I believe that I'll be making a difference."

"That's always a good thing. Just promise me that you'll be careful."

I promise to be as careful as I can be. How's that?"

"I know you're grown and all that, but you're still my baby boy!"

Travis blushes when his mom says things like that. He's a grown man, but she can make him feel like a small boy. This brings a smile to his face. In her eyes, he will always be her little boy. Travis feels more loved in this moment than he has since Sarah and Jamie were alive.

He knew his mom wanted to ask him about Sarah and Jamie, but she didn't want to upset him by bringing it up. He would talk to them about it later. He knew his mom and dad were hurting just as badly as he was. He wanted to make sure they were all right also.

They arrive at his parent's home and everyone goes inside. His mom takes him in his old room and tells him to settle in and she will prepare them all some lunch. Travis stands in his old room and is amazed that his mom hasn't changed a single thing since he left home.

Travis puts his bags away and goes to find his dad. He finds him in his workshop out back.

"So Dad, who fixes the roof for you now when you shoot at the snakes?"

His dad laughs and tells him that his brother does. Travis has fond memories in this shop - the time that he and his dad spent out here; the projects they worked on together. This is where he taught Travis how to work on cars and how to build things.

"So Dad, how are you and Mom doing? Really."

"We're doing ok. We miss you and Sarah and Jamie something awful, but we get by with memories."

"I know it's been tough on y'all. I hate that I haven't been to see you since the funeral. Just trying to adjust and start the new job."

"Your Mom and I understand. We can only imagine how hard it's been on you. It's probably a good thing that you have a new job to concentrate on instead of dwelling on what happened. We knew you would come when the time was right."

"It really has helped concentrating on work and keeping my mind on something else. I think about you and Mom all the time and wonder how you're feeling. I know how much you and Mom loved Sarah and Jamie. I can only imagine how tough it's been on y'all."

"Hey you guys, lunch is ready."

Travis and his dad head into the house to enjoy lunch together. His dad is such a strong man, and Travis has all the respect in the world for him. His mom has laid out a small feast. That's the southern woman in her. She has homemade chicken salad with fresh fruit and sweet tea. There are all kinds of fresh desserts as well as fresh vegetables. Travis stuffs his face like he hasn't eaten in a month. No one can feed him like his mom. Travis looks at her.

"Ok, let's address the 400 pound elephant in the room. I'm sorry that I haven't been home since the funeral. I know that you and Dad have been hurting about Sarah and Jamie. I've just been taking some time to process the whole thing. I'm lucky I have my new job to keep me occupied. I know you miss Sarah and Jamie and I know how much you cared for and loved them. I just wish that I could have been here for the two of you."

"Honey, it's ok. We understand. You needed time to heal as well as did we. I know it's probably hard for you to talk about it. Just know that your Dad and I are here for you. We know you're here for us as well. I'm glad that you have something that takes your mind off of it. Your Dad and I have each other to lean on. You're bearing all the weight by yourself. You know Daddy and I are here for you when you need us."

"I know, Mom. I know that y'all will always be here when I need you. You have no idea how much that thought has helped me get through all this."

Travis sees tears in his mom's eyes, and he sees tears in his dad's eyes also. This in turn brings tears to Travis's eyes. Travis clears his throat and looks at his parents with love and admiration.

"Ok, now that that's out of the way, what are we going to do this afternoon?"

"I have to go to the course and water the greens."

"How about if Mom and I come along and we do some fishing at the pond on number 18 fairway like we used to?"

"That sounds like a plan."

"Mom, you still have that lucky safety pin that you always use to catch more fish with than me and Dad?"

They finish lunch and Travis helps his mom clean up. They all pile into the car and head to the country club. His dad built this golf course years ago with shovels and a tractor. Travis loves this place. It seems like it's always been home for him. His dad is the superintendent and protects this course with a vengeance. Travis grew up on this course and used to work with his dad when he got old enough. It truly was like coming home.

"I'll get Mom set up and ready to fish while you go start watering the greens. When you get done, join us and we'll fish the day away."

Travis and his mom start fishing while his dad waters the greens. Travis doesn't get to do much fishing because his mom keeps pulling them out faster than Travis can take them off. Travis laughs about this. He remembers his mom fishing with a brass safety pin with no bait, and she would catch more fish than he and his dad put together. She had to be the luckiest fisherman in the world. He and his dad had tried her trick and it never worked for them.

Travis thought about his dad. He was always a hardworking man with integrity, and he was content with the simple things in life. As long as he had a roof over his family's head and enough money, he was a happy man. He never needed the finer things in life. Just work, family and enough to get by. He had instilled these values in Travis, and Travis was happy with that.

Travis and his mom had been fishing for a couple of hours when his dad joined them. They all just sat back and relaxed for the rest of the afternoon. Around dark they packed up and headed home for a good night's rest.

FIFTY

Travis rises early the next morning only to find that his dad has already gone to work, and his mom is making his breakfast. He shouldn't be surprised. It has been this way all of his life. The phone rings and Travis's Mom answers.

"Hello."

"Is Travis there?"

"Yes he is, hold on a minute and I'll get him for you."

"Hello."

"Travis, this is Director Turner."

"What can I do for you, Director?"

"I hate to bother you when you're trying to relax, but I have uncovered some things you need to look at and you're not going to like what you see."

"What's it pertaining to?"

"Your team. Or should I say, certain members of your team. I need to come see you immediately. Can you meet me at the airport?"

"Yes, I can. What time will you be arriving?"

"I'll be leaving here when I hang up. Give me about three hours to get there."

"I'll see you then."

Travis hangs up the phone and tells his mom that he needs to go to the airport to meet his boss. Something has come up. His mom understands and asks if he'll be coming back or if he'll have to leave. Travis tells her he'll let her know as soon as he finds out what the problem is. Travis calls a cab and heads to the airport in Raleigh.

Travis arrives at the airport and waits for Turner at the private jet terminal. Travis sees the jet arrive and taxi into the terminal.

"Hello, Travis. I'm sorry that I have to bother you, but I feel you need to see this asap."

"That's ok, Director. I know you wouldn't come see me if it weren't important. So, what have you got?"

"Squeaker came to me with some information he dug up doing a routine scan of the comms. He found there was a call placed to Columbia from inside the Op's Center. It matched a number that we got from tracing Joanne's phone calls. Someone inside the Op's Center had to have placed that call. All the lines going to the Op's Center are dedicated. Nothing from the outside can interfere with those lines. Just the way you asked for them to be. It was really smart on your part to have Squeaker run checks on those lines without anybody else knowing."

"Things like this are why I had him do that without anybody's knowledge, including yours. That pretty much clears Squeaker. Now we have to figure out who placed that call and why. It's hard for me to believe that one of my guys would do something like this. I trust these guys with my life each and every day."

"I know Travis, that's why I'm here. We don't know who did it, and we don't know what was said. But whatever it is can't be good."

"I agree 100 percent. I have a feeling I know why and what. The why is money and greed. The what is probably getting locations to a hit team. I need to protect my family, but not sure who to bring down to do it."

"Don't you worry about that. I'll have a couple of teams come down that I know aren't involved in any of this. We'll secure your family. You need to figure this out and figure it out quickly. What do you have in mind?"

"If it's to give locations, then I'll come back to the Op's Center and force whoever made the call to call them again and let them know I'm back in DC. Then we'll have who's responsible and I'll deal with them my way."

"That's probably the best way to try and flush them out. No one knows I'm here. No one knows about the comms sweep except you, Squeaker and me. They're probably feeling safe about being able to call whenever they need to."

"That's what I'm thinking. I'll have you contact Squeaker and have him monitor all the lines. We'll see where the call is made from and who's in that area at the time the call is made. I'll need to have Walbach run financials on each member of the team and look for any offshore accounts coming back to them. This includes Squeaker too - just to be fair and safe."

"I'll have him start on that as soon as we get back. I'm really sorry I had to interrupt your trip."

"Don't worry about that. You did the right thing by coming. I'll have to call my family and let them know what to expect. If I don't, my Dad will shoot anybody hanging around the house that he doesn't know about. I'll be back after I make that call."

Travis goes to the phones and calls his mom. His dad is home for lunch, so Travis talks to him and lets him know what's going on and what to expect. He tells his parents that he loves them, and that he'll be in touch soon. Travis returns and meets up with Turner. They board the plane and head back to DC.

FIFTY-ONE

Langley Op's Center

Travis and the director land in DC and head back to the Op's Center. Travis and Turner meet with Agent Walbach and fill him in on what they need him to do. Director Turner makes a call and has two teams head out to North Carolina with instructions on what's happening and what they need to take care of while there.

Travis shows up at the Op's Center and throws everybody off balance with his sudden appearance.

"Why's everybody so shocked to see me here?"

"We all thought you'd be gone for a few more days."

"You know I can't stay away from you guys more than a couple of days at a time."

Everyone laughs and the tension is broken. That's why Travis is a good leader for this team. He makes everyone feel at ease and feel like family.

Only, now one of them is no longer a part of that family.

"Where's Muskrat?"

"He decided to take a couple days off while you were gone to see his family."

"Ok. Squeaker, I need to see you in my office."

"Sure Skipper, what's up?"

"I'm back because of what you found during the comm sweep. When did Muskrat leave to go home?"

"Right after you left, Skipper."

"Where was that call made from in the Op's Center?"

"It was made from the computer room."

"Who was in the computer room when the call was made? Do we know that?"

"I know that Muskrat, Falcon and Merlin were all in the computer room close to the time that the call was made."

"Ok. I want you to monitor all channels in and out of here twenty-four seven, until we see another call made to that number. I want to know immediately when it is and where it's made from."

"Roger that, Skipper."

"I want you to call Muskrat and let him know I'm back. I want you to monitor his home phone until he's back in the Op's Center. We clear on that?"

"Roger, Skipper. We're clear on that."

"Let me know when you contact him. I'll be in my office or with Director Turner. Just so you know, I'll be checking into each team member until we find who made that call. Thank you for the work you've done. I know it's hard to suspect that someone on this team is a bad seed. It makes me sick to think about it. But we have to remain vigilant until we do. Understand?"

"I do understand, Skipper. I'll keep this to myself until we know for sure."

"Thank you, Squeaker."

Travis returns to his office to try to wrap his head around the idea that someone in his family of brothers could do such a thing to him or anybody else on the team. Who and where did someone get their claws into one of his team? Travis thinks about when his team had exposure to anyone that could have swayed them. He was coming up with a blank.

"Skipper, I just wanted to let you know that I got in touch with Muskrat and he'll be in first thing tomorrow."

"Thanks, Squeaker. What did he say when you told him I was back?"

"All he said was 'oh shit', and then he said he would be back tomorrow."

Travis hangs up and thinks about Muskrat and all the time they had spent together. What could possibly make Muskrat turn? Hell, what could make any of them turn for that matter? They had been through Hell and back together and each one trusted the other with his life. Travis didn't like the feeling he was getting from this.

Director Turner calls Travis and asks him to come to his office.

"Come on in, Travis, I have someone I want you to meet. Travis, this is Assistant Director Chuck Smith. Chuck, this is Travis Bones."

"Travis, it's good to finally meet you. I have heard nothing but good things about you."

"Thank you, Mr. Smith."

"Please call me Chuck."

"All right, Chuck. To what do I owe the honor of meeting you?"

"Director Turner will be going out of town on personal business and I'll be handling the situation until he gets back."

"When will you be leaving, Director?"

"Tonight right after this meeting. Chuck is up to speed on everything that's happening with the situation, including with your family."

"Chuck, do you have any questions?"

"No, but I would like to sit down with you and get your take on things - if you have the time."

"That would be fine."

"Gentlemen, if you don't mind, I'll go ahead and take my leave and let you two discuss whatever you need to talk about. Feel free to use my office for as long as you need."

"Thank you, Peter. I think we'll take this to my office."

Director Turner leaves and Chuck and Travis make their way to Chuck's office.

"So Travis, I understand that you were responsible for bringing down Senator Baker and his wife Joanne."

"Yes Sir, I was. I got lucky and figured it out before they could do anything about it. Believe me, they tried."

"So I understand. I also understand that it was not luck that you figured things out. Director Turner speaks very highly of you."

"Thank you, Chuck. I just took the information I was given and did what I was trained to do with it."

"I think you're going to have a long and very successful career with the agency. I read your test scores and I can honestly say I have never seen anything even remotely close to what you scored. It's going to be a pleasure working with you."

"Thank you again, Chuck. I give all the credit to my parents and family for teaching me to never stop learning and giving me the ability to put that knowledge to good use."

"So what do you think is happening with your team, and do you think there's more than one member involved?"

"I personally can't wrap my mind around the idea that one of my guys could do such a thing. I know I have to be realistic about the situation, but something is just not adding up."

"Do you have any theories as to what might have happened and how it came to be?"

"The only thing that makes sense is that somehow, somewhere, someone got to one of the group. But the problem with that theory is the fact that we have run over 300 missions together and I know these boys better than I know some of my family. I just can't come up with anything that would make one of them turn on the rest of us."

"What makes you think it was one of the guys?"

"There were only three members in the room where the call was placed. Those are dedicated lines and cannot be manipulated from outside of the Op's Center."

"You know anything can be breached. Hell, you do it for a living. Getting in where you're not supposed to get in. Suppose it wasn't breached in the Op's Center. Maybe it was breached before it got to the Op's Center."

"If that were the case, then it wouldn't have shown up on the comm sweep. Anything done before the Op's Center is dedicated also. It wouldn't have come to the Op's Center. It would show up on the telephone companies' logs, but not ours. It had to be done inside the Op's Center."

"You're sure that no one else had access to that room during that time?"

"I was gone at the time it happened, but from what my guys are saying, no one else was in the Op's Center but team members. Just to be sure, I'll have Squeaker run a log on the entry door access pad for that day."

"I doubt anything will show up, but you never know. Maybe the team was preoccupied and didn't notice someone else in the Op's Center."

"Hell, at this point I'm open to anything."

"I would like to have Agent Walbach pull the jackets of all team members, including myself, and rerun background and financial checks."

FIFTY-TWO

Langley Op's Center

Travis goes down to the Op's Center and calls a team meeting.

"Ok, men. We have a situation. It's not one that I'm comfortable with, and it's one you won't be comfortable with. With that being said, we have a breach in security. I don't know how, but we do. Someone placed a call from the computer room, and according to the logs, only three team members were in the room around the time the call was made. You all know how I feel about you. You're my brothers and I love all of you. That's what makes this so difficult for me. I truly do not believe that anyone in this room did anything but their duties. However, as per protocol, each member will have his jacket double checked, including myself, and backgrounds will have to be rechecked. It's not comfortable for me and I'm sure it won't be for you either."

"Skipper, why are you checking yourself? You weren't even here at the time it happened. We understand about the team being checked; we were here, but not you."

"I'm a member of this team, and as such, I'm subject to the same rules that everyone else is. I will not be the one doing the checks. I have asked Agent Walbach to do the checks. That way, there can be no hint of impropriety. We have been through Hell and back together many times. I believe in my heart that we all will be vindicated in the end. It's a process that has to be done and we'll make the best of it."

"Skipper, we are with you 100 percent."

"I'm glad to hear you say that. I didn't expect anything less from you guys. Squeaker, I need you to pull a log for the entry door the day this occurred. I want to know if anyone other than team members were in the Op's Center that day."

"Roger, Skipper. I can have that for you in about two hours."

"Good. We'll all go about our duties as normal. I want nothing to change. Dismissed."

The team starts going about their duties as expected. Travis walks to his office and waits for the door log. He sits back and contemplates about how someone could have gotten in the Op's Center without being seen.

"Skipper, I have the door logs you asked for."

"Come on in, Squeaker. What have you found?"

"I came up with one anomaly. You're not going to like who it is."

"Is it someone not on the team?"

"Sort of."

"What do you mean, sort of?"

"He's not a direct team member, but he's associated with the team."

Travis looks at the logs and can't believe his eyes. Never in a million years would he have guessed this name. It has to be a mistake. Travis looks at Squeaker with rage in his eyes.

"Squeaker, did this person enter the computer room?"

"Yes sir, Skipper. About two minutes before the call was made."

"I need to go see Assistant Director Smith right away."

Travis takes off upstairs to the Assistant Director's office. Assistant Director Smith isn't in his office when Travis arrives. Travis decides to sit and wait for him to return. Travis's mind is reeling. He can't believe the name that showed up on the log. If what he suspects is true, the entire agency could be in jeopardy.

"Travis, I hope you haven't been waiting too long."

"No Sir, but I have something I think you need to see."

Travis shows Assistant Director Smith the door log for the entry and computer room door.

"You're certain this is accurate?"

"Yes, Sir. There's no doubt. This system was put into place to track things such as this kind of anomaly."

"What do you propose we do?"

"I think the first thing we need to do is talk to the President and get his take on the situation."

"Let me make a call and see what I can set up. I'll let you know as soon as I can get something arranged."

"Thank you, Sir. In the meantime, I'll talk to Agent Walbach and have him stop the checks on the team and run checks on this person instead. My team and I will do some checking of our own also."

Travis returns to Agent Walbach's office to let him know about the change of plans. Travis goes back down to the Op's Center to get started and wait to hear from Assistant Director Smith.

"Gentlemen, we need to do a deep dive into this person. We need to find out everything we can including what he had for breakfast this morning. Is everyone clear on this?"

"Roger, Skipper."

"I want no stone left unturned. If what I suspect is true, time is of the essence. I want a full rundown - personal, financial and anything else we can come up with. Be ready to deploy on my word. We have a major security breach here and the sooner we plug it, the better off we'll be."

"Roger, Skipper."

"Do it!"

Travis goes to his office and waits for the call from Smith. If this is true, Carpenter can kiss re-election goodbye. Hell, everybody might kiss their careers goodbye. As Travis is contemplating his next move, the phone rings.

"Travis, I have a meeting set for seven pm tonight. You can ride with me."

"I'll meet you upstairs beforehand. I'll hopefully have more information by that time."

"Come to my office about six and we'll go from there."

Travis shows up at Assistant Director Smith's office at five minutes to six. They both move downstairs for the ride to the White House. When they're in the car and traveling to their appointment, Travis shows Smith what they've found since they last talked.

FIFTY-THREE

Oval Office – The White House

Travis and Assistant Director Smith discuss the findings on the ride over. As they approach the White House, Travis lets Smith in on what he intends to ask the President. They arrive and wait in the Oval Office for the President's arrival.

"Hello, Chuck. Hello, Travis. Please be seated and tell me what you've found. You're going to have to have cold hard facts if you intend to expect me to make a major decision at this stage of the game. You know after everything that has happened, I stand next to no chance of being re-elected. It'll take a lot for me to make a move on a major player at this point."

"Well Mr. President, if you look at the facts and listen to what Travis has to say, you might not have to make that decision. Travis has a unique solution for this problem that just might make your re-election a little less hard to pull off."

"Hell son, if you can pull that off, I'll sign off on anything you want at this point. Not really, but

I'm most interested in listening to what you have to say. Travis, the floor is yours."

"Thank you, Mr. President. As you're well aware, the last thing you need right now is another scandal. We have a rogue agent at the CIA. He can bring a lot of heat down on you at the moment. If you allow me and my team to bring this to a conclusion for you, we can make it look like an assassination by a foreign government or radical party from that country, and we can make the rest look like you're the President who's cleaning up a corrupt government. That will go a long way towards helping you secure re-election."

"You definitely have my undivided attention. How do you propose to accomplish this magical solution?"

"Well Mr. President, first you need to look at the evidence that we have against this agent. Once you do that, I'll lay out our plan to right the ship."

"Ok. Let's see what you have."

Travis hands the documents over to the President. The President looks them over and grows increasingly disturbed.

"I don't see how in the Hell you'll be able to take this and turn it into a positive situation, Travis."

"That's the beauty of this plan, Mr. President. You'll come out smelling like a rose and the country will be pissed off that a foreign group would have the nerve to try and pull something like this off. If you give the word to retaliate against those responsible, that will boost your stock with the general public and make them feel like you're a President who won't stand by and let someone do something against the United States and get by with it."

"Do I really want to know what you're planning, or will I be better served not knowing?"

"Personally Sir, I think plausible deniability is the best route for you to take. We'll run the operation and take care of the problem. All you have to do is believe us when we tell you who's responsible and give the word for us to take care of the perpetrators. That way, the problem is solved, and we can eliminate a problem group we wouldn't normally have reason to go after."

"You make it sound so simple. What kind of guarantee do I have that this will work the way you say it will?"

"You just have to trust the professionalism of my team and me to do what we say we can do, Sir."

"Hell, at this point what do I have to lose? Make it happen and may God be with you on this one."

"Thank you, Mr. President. Once all is said and done, if you want to know the particulars of the mission, I'll be more than happy to give them to you, Sir."

"If you pull this off, you can write your own ticket. I will probably never want to know how you did it."

Everyone laughs and Travis and Assistant Director Smith head back to Langley to set things in motion.

FIFTY-FOUR

Langley Op's Center

Travis and Smith arrive back at Langley. Smith goes to his office to arrange transportation for the mission. Travis goes down to the Op's Center to brief the team.

"Gentlemen, we have a hard target. We'll be going into this with no prep time and not knowing exactly the parameters of our target. We don't know what he'll be doing, or where in the building he will be exactly. We don't have the luxury of recon on this particular target. We'll get in, take out the target, and get out without being seen or heard. Any locals or innocents will be tranquilized and not harmed. Are we clear on this?"

"Roger, Skipper."

"We'll be doing a halo jump into the area with a rooftop landing, so everyone needs to be heads up on this. We can't afford to have anyone hurt on the landing. Understood?"

"Understood, Skipper."

"Good. Be ready and staged at 11:00 hours."

Travis and the team are ready at the appointed time. They assemble and load up for the ride to Andrews. When they arrive they board the C-130 on the tarmac. This will be a long and bumpy flight so they'll rest on the way. There'll be no rest once they arrive. The flight will be 12 hours with in-air refueling. The destination is Brasilia, Brazil. The team will be landing on the roof of the San Marco Hotel. It's in a noisy section of the city which will help hide the landing. They have managed to come up with the original specs for the hotel. According to sources inside the country, there have been no renovations done to the building since it was built in the 60's. At least Travis and the team will have basic intel. They settle in for the long flight.

FIFTY-FIVE

Brasilia, Brazil

Travis and the team make last minute equipment checks. They're five minutes out from the jump. They'll jump from 30,000 feet and free fall till 2,000 feet before deploying the chutes. It'll be an extremely hard landing. It'll be a night landing on a rooftop they're not familiar with. Travis and his team stage at the rear of the aircraft and prepare to jump.

The ramp lowers and Travis and team jump into the empty abyss of the night sky. Travis and his team rocket toward the unknown situation on the ground. The team watches their wrist altimeters and at 2,000 feet they separate and deploy their chutes. As the chutes open one by one, the team releases their tether straps for their equipment bags.

One by one they all land on the roof with no problems. They gather their chutes and stash them on the roof, so the wind doesn't bother them. They gear up and form up on Travis. Spider will the first one over the wall. He'll locate the target and the best route in. Genius will find entrance into the building from the roof. Falcon has rooftop duty, directing what the locals are doing. Trojan will be ready with any diversions needed. Guardian will be on the insertion team in case any locals get in the way. Merlin will be on the insertion team in case any magic needs to happen. Boomer and Muskrat are on the insertion team. Beaver will make his way to ground level in case an alternate path of escape is needed. Brutus will be on the insertion team to take out anybody needing to be dealt with. Squeaker will be doing what Squeaker does best - monitoring everything. Details are set. Time to execute.

Spider goes over the side and starts searching for the target. Genius is in the process of gaining entry to the hotel interior. The rest are waiting on Spider. Spider radios Squeaker and the others. Target has been acquired. He's on the top floor in the center room on the west side of the building. Time to go to work. Genius gains access to the top floor. The insertion team makes entry.

"Check the hallway."

"There's one guard on the door."

"Tranquilize his ass and get him out of sight."

"Roger that, Skipper. He's down and out of sight."

"Check the rest of the hallways."

"Everything's clear, Skipper."

"Prepare to breach the door on my command. Spider, how many guards inside?"

"I see no guards inside, Skipper."

"Breach on one. Three, two, one."

The team breaches the door and secures the entryway to the room. Travis enters the room.

"Travis, what in the Hell do you think you're doing?"

"Correcting a mighty damn big wrong. You try and set me and my team up, you better damn well be ready for the consequences."

"What the Hell are you talking about, set you and your team up? Set you up for what?"

"Don't play stupid with me. You know me better than that. I wouldn't be here if I didn't have proof to back up what I said."

"I have no idea what you're talking about."

"Is that really the way you want to play this? Really? We know it was you who placed the phone call to Columbia. What I want to know is why? Who got to you?"

"No one got to me. I went to them. You're worth a lot of money to the right person. I made sure that Joanne made it worth my effort. I guess I should have known you would figure it out. I just figure I would be gone and untouchable by the time you did. You had to clear yourself and your team's name first."

"That didn't take much to do. You should have planned better."

"So, what happens now? You take me in and create another scandal for the President? Do you really think he's going to let that happen?"

"No, I don't. You see, this is going to play out a little different than what you might think."

"What the Hell do you mean, differently?"

"I mean permanently."

"You think you can just come into a foreign country and kill me and get by with it? You must be insane."

"We're the CIA. We've been doing this sort of thing for years. I not only can, but will, and there's not a damn thing you can do about it."

"Does the President know you're here?"

"Do you think I would be doing something like this without the blessing of the man you're trying to destroy?"

"How do you plan on pulling this off?"

"Sit down and let me tell you a little story. You'll be killed by a radical group from Brazil that hates the United States. That will garner sympathy for the President. He in turn will retaliate against said group for the atrocities committed against the United States. This will in turn earn him support in the polls and help him win re-election."

"He's so far behind in the polls that he can't possibly win the election."

"That, my friend, is where you're wrong. He will be seen as the President that's cleaning up the corrupt government."

"You really are smarter than I gave you credit for. Hell, this just might work. Let me come back and help you with this."

"If you come back, then this won't work. You're the catalyst for this whole damn plan. If you're not assassinated, then he has no reason to retaliate. Do you really think I would work with you after what you tried to do to me and my team? You're not as smart as I thought you were."

"I can make it worth your while to let me escape. I'll stay out of sight and not cause you any problems."

"Begging is not becoming of a man of your stature. Do I look stupid enough to fall for your bullshit?"

"No, I guess not."

"At least your name won't be smeared as a result of your assassination. Goodbye, Director."

Travis raises his pistol and pumps two rounds into his forehead. The Director slumps over on the couch. Travis and his team leave the room and drive to the airport. They'll take commercial flights back to DC using alias names.

FIFTY-SIX

Washington DC

"Breaking News. This is Cory Stevens reporting for NBC News from Washington, DC. CIA Director Peter Turner was found assassinated in his room at the San Marco Hotel in Brasilia, Brazil, this morning. It's believed that he was there on official business. No one has come forward to claim responsibility as of this broadcast. The President is expected to hold a press conference later today. We'll cover the press conference live as it happens. We now return you to your regular programming."

"Welcome to the Op's Center, Mr. President."

"Thank you, Travis. You boys pulled it off without a hitch. I must commend you on a job well done. Now Travis, if we could get together in private to discuss what I'll be saying in my press conference later."

"Yes sir, Mr. President, if you will join me in my office. Chuck, we'll need you also."

"You fellows did a Hell of a job on this assignment. Now tell me what I need to say to the public."

"First, you need to express your sadness at what has happened. Then you need to show your passion and rage at what has transpired. Tell them we know who did this and they will be dealt with. Then you need to announce that Chuck Smith will be appointed as the new Director of the CIA. Now let's get you back to the White House and ready for your press conference"

"This is Cory Stevens with NBC News. We're going live to the White House where President Carpenter will be holding a press conference about the events that unfolded this morning concerning CIA Director Peter Turner."

"Good morning, everyone. It's with a heavy heart that I come before you this morning to announce that CIA Director Peter Turner was found assassinated in his hotel room this morning in Brasilia, Brazil. We have an active investigation going on in this matter. I'm not at liberty to discuss any details at this time. I'll not be announcing who this person is, but at this time we are in the process of putting together a joint operation with the Brazilian government that will bring a swift and permanent resolution to this tragedy.

Let it be known that the United States of America will not tolerate, nor will we stand idly by, as things such as this happen to American citizens. We'll deal with this threat to America's safety as a proud nation. Director Turner has served this nation proudly for over 30 years, and his death will not be taken lightly. I pledge to you that within 72 hours, this situation will be resolved, and it will be done forcefully and with impunity to those responsible. We'll make a statement that every nation on this planet will understand. Do not rebel against The United States of America. I'll personally oversee this action to its conclusion.

As you all are aware, we have another situation in this country now as well - that of corrupt government officials. I will not tolerate this either. I'll root out all those involved and bring them to justice. This cannot and will not be tolerated in our great country. The people of our country have elected these officials to work on their behalf and by God, that is what will happen. Those that choose to use this position for personal gain will not be tolerated by this administration. They'll be brought before the courts and receive the justice that America demands.

I must announce at this time that Assistant Director Chuck Smith of the CIA will be named the new Director of the CIA. Chuck has spent over 20 years serving his country with dignity and strength. He'll make a fine Director for this agency. Thank you all for coming. Good morning. I will not be taking questions at this time."

FIFTY-SEVEN

The White House – Oval Office

Travis waits in the Oval Office for the President and Director Smith to finish the press conference and join him.

President Carpenter and the director join Travis.

"How did the press conference go?"

"It went very well. There seems to be a lot of support to seek revenge for Turner's death."

"Good. I've been looking at the poll numbers while the press conference was going on. According to the latest numbers, you seem to be back on top in the polls. Mr. President, you're ahead by ten points in all the polls."

"I swear Travis, if you manage to pull this off for me, you can write your own ticket for you and your team. You can never know how much your support and help in this matter means to me."

"Well Mr. President, this is a win for everybody, but especially for the American people, Sir."

"I just hope you're right about this. Enough about me, let's get down to discussing how we're going to deal with this whole situation in Brazil. Chuck, what are your thoughts on the matter?"

"With all due respect, Mr. President, I'm going to defer to Travis and his team on this whole idea. They're the masterminds when it comes to pulling this off."

"I agree with you, Chuck. Ok Travis, what have you and the boys come up with?"

"Well, Sir, who's the biggest pain in the ass for the United States in Brazil right now?"

"That would be the Partido Dos Trabalhadores group. They're trying to stage a coup and influence the vote down there right now."

"Exactly, Sir. My team will go down to Brazil under the guise of escorting Turner's body back to the United States for burial. While we're there, we'll locate and take out the leaders of the Partido Dos Trabalhadores and any significant players on the side lines. This'll be a win for Brazil and for the United States interests in Brazil. I assume you've talked to the Brazilian Government?"

"I have and they're on board with us as to dealing with the people responsible for this tragedy. They wish to remain on the good side of the U.S. on this one. Besides, we take care of a problem for them also."

"Have you given them a name as to who's responsible yet?"

"Not yet. But I'll make that call when we finish up here."

"Good deal, Sir. We can spend a couple of days doing recon and then on the day we leave for the U.S. with the body, we take them out and leave. No one will be the wiser and we get our revenge."

"That sounds like a good idea. Do we have any intelligence on where this group is located?"

"Yes Sir, we do. They have several small groups located around the area, but the main group tied to the leaders operates out of Brasilia. They do this to gain an advantage on their enemies. They believe in the whole 'Keep your friends close, but your enemies even closer' concept. They're well armed and train on a regular basis."

"How do you propose to get to them unseen?"

"Leave that to me and the team, Sir. If you can arrange a contact for us within the government that has real time knowledge of the group and their strongholds, that would be most useful to us. Someone who has eyes and ears on the group."

"I'll make arrangements and get that information to you."

"My team and I will leave in a few hours. We'll get in country sometime in the morning. Arrange for the body to be ready for shipment in three days. That'll give us enough time to recon and execute our plan. I know you and the Director have more business to discuss, so I'll take my leave now and get back to Langley to prepare. I'll wait for your call, Mr. President."

"Thank you, Travis. I'll call you soon with the details."

Travis leaves and makes his way back to the Op's Center to brief the team and awaits the President's call.

FIFTY-EIGHT

Brasilia, Brazil

Travis and his team receive the information from the President and board the C-130 Hercules for Brasilia. The President has made arrangements for the team to stay at the military leader's home. That way, he can vouch for the team if any questions come up.

Travis and the team arrive just after eight in the morning. They're met at the airport by General Carlos Ramos, head of the Brazilian military. They'll be staying at his home while they're in Brazil.

Travis and General Ramos discuss military tactics on the ride to Ramos's home. The General is very interested in picking Travis's brain about such matters in hopes of gaining new insights that he can use for his own army.

They arrive at General Ramos's home. Travis is surprised to find that General Ramos has a scale model of the Partido Dos Trabalhadores camp in Brasilia. This will without a doubt help Travis and his team.

"This will definitely help us with the raid, General."

"I'm glad to hear this, Travis."

"Carlos, if we're successful with this raid, I promise you that I'll come back with my team and teach your guys special tactics and weapons in exchange for your help in this."

"Thank you Travis; that will be very much appreciated. I'll look forward to it. I know you'll be successful. Hopefully this will help you."

"This will help more than you know, Carlos. I wish we had this kind of intel on all operations."

"I have one small favor to ask, if I may."

"What might that be, Carlos?"

"I very much wish to observe the operation in action. I know I won't be involved, but might I ask permission to observe from a distance."

"I feel sure we can make that happen. How about if you observe from atop this hill? That should give you a good position to see everything that goes on."

"Wonderful. Thank you very much."

Travis and Carlos talk into the night and finally realize it has gotten late and they've had quite a bit to drink. Travis excuses himself and goes to bed.

Travis rises the next morning and has General Ramos take him and the team on a ride past the camp. They stop on the hill that General Ramos will be observing from so he can get a bird's eye view of the compound.

"Travis, you must understand that I have a man on the inside of the compound. I must tell him when the raid will happen so he can get out before it all goes down. He's a good man and I don't want him to get hurt."

"Carlos, I'm afraid I can't have those kinds of details released before the raid. I'm sure you understand. If you provide my team with pictures of this man, I assure you he won't be harmed by us."

"I understand. I'll make sure your team has pictures of my guy inside."

"I can't promise that they won't shoot him. Do they have any idea that he's your man?"

"None whatsoever. He's been with them for over a year now. They trust him."

"Is there any way that we could talk to him before we go in?"

"Yes, I can arrange for you to meet him this afternoon."

"That would be perfect. Does he know anything about the raid yet?"

"I haven't told him anything. I was waiting until you arrived to let him know."

"Good. I'll handle how much he's told and when."

Travis and the team spend an hour watching the camp and the activities happening inside. Travis decides to leave a couple of team members on the hilltop to observe the camp. He'll rotate the guys in and out so that they can keep watch twenty-four seven until it's time for the raid.

"Boomer and Falcon, you have first watch. I'll have someone on comms at all times in case they decide to do something, or you need to let us know something. The rest of you guys head back and get some rest. Trojan and Muskrat will relieve you at 18:00 hours. Carlos, if you can arrange that meeting with your man inside, I'll wait to hear from you."

"I'll call as soon as I find out anything."

Travis and the guys head back to the General's house to rest and prepare for what they plan to do. Travis studies the model of the camp in the General's house and struggles to lay out a mission plan. The General calls Travis and tells him they have a meeting set up for 16:00 hours. Travis continues to study the model until time.

"Hello, Travis. This is Jose Hernandez. He's my contact inside the camp."

"Thank you, Carlos. I'm very pleased to meet you, Jose. Let's get down to business. Exactly where are the leader's quarters and what kind of schedule do they have?"

"The leaders stay in these buildings here. Everyone goes to eat at seven o'clock in the evening. That's when they're the most vulnerable. That's when everyone's relaxed and talking and eating and not paying much attention to anything else. Jose points out each building as he's explaining things to Travis"

"Where does everyone gather?"

"In this building here. Everyone eats at the same time "

"Are any guards posted while they eat?"

"Yes, usually three guards. One is stationed here, one here and the other one here."

"Does the location of the guards ever change for any reason?"

"No. The same place every day at mealtime."

"How heavily are they armed?"

"The guards always carry AK-47s. Each guard also carries grenades and a pistol."

"You're sure that they're always at the same place during the meal?'

"Yes, always the same place."

"Is the perimeter of the camp booby trapped?"

"Yes, it is. All except the back fence that butts up against the hillside. There's nothing on this fence."

"How are the fences rigged?"

"The other three fences have trip wires set to claymore mines. They're rigged so that if the fence is cut, flares will launch to let them know where the intruders are coming from."

"Do you know how to undo the trip wires?"

"No. This I know nothing about. I have no training in anything like that."

"Ok. Are there guards on duty continuously at night?"

"Yes. They always have three guards on duty. The guards in the middle of the camp are in a tower. They have a machine gun as well as spotlights to sweep the camp with at night."

"How often do they sweep the camp with the lights?"

"They constantly sweep the camp, but there's only one light, so they can't cover the whole camp at the same time."

"Is there anything else that we need to know about night routines in the camp?"

"The leader, Manuel Ortiz, gets up all hours of the night and walks around. He's always expecting something to happen and doesn't trust many people."

"Are there any particular times he roams around?"

"No. He always makes sure that it's at different times. He says that this way, no one will know exactly when he'll be doing it and they can't surprise him this way. Manuel is very paranoid."

"Manuel should be paranoid. When you do the kinds of things he does, you need to worry that someone will come to get you."

"Yes, this I know for a fact."

All three men laugh at this.

"Jose, I can't thank you enough for the information you've provided. I can't tell you the time or day when we'll strike but rest assured that my men will protect you. All you have to do is stay inside and you will not be harmed. Show me which building you're in at night and I'll have my men protect that building."

"I'm always in this building at night. There are five other men in this building with me. There are six men in all of these buildings here."

"When you hear anything happening at night, keep your head down and we'll protect you."

"Thank you, Travis. I must be getting back before they suspect anything."

"I understand. Thank you again, Jose."

Travis returns to studying the model of the camp and making his game plan. He knows more now, and that information is priceless when it comes to missions like this. Travis spends the next three hours putting together his plan.

Travis completes his plan and leaves to take a look firsthand at the camp once more before finalizing the details. Travis takes off with Trojan and Muskrat.

Travis and the guys arrive just in time to see a truck pull in and the men in camp start unloading crates that look suspiciously like weapons crates. Travis grabs his binoculars and looks more closely. Sure enough, the crates are marked as M72 Laws Rockets - a handheld, shoulder fired 66-mm unguided anti-tank system used by the United States Military. How in the Hell they managed to get their hands on those is anyone's guess.

"We'll need to keep an eye on those and see where they store them. We'll take those with us when we complete the raid on the camp. I don't want those getting into the wrong hands."

"Roger that, Skipper. We don't want those hanging around after we leave."

"No, we do not. Make sure we keep tabs on them. I can only imagine what they have planned for those."

Travis and the guys spend the next several hours tracking the movements inside the camp and making notes. They get positive identification on the leaders and where they're staying. Everything checks with what Jose has told Travis. This makes Travis feel a whole lot better about everything. Travis sees Jose walking around the camp talking and laughing with the others. Travis stays until about 02:30, then leaves for the General's house.

Travis rises early the next morning and joins the guys at breakfast.

"After breakfast, everyone meet in the study for mission planning. We'll be going tonight at 02:30."

Travis and the guys finish breakfast and gather in the study to wait for General Ramos's arrival.

"All right, everyone's here now. Let's begin. We'll strike at 02:30. General Ramos, you'll be on the hilltop with me as overwatch. I can always use an extra set of eyes.

Genius, you'll secure the M72 rockets.

Falcon, track any aircraft in the area. General Ramos will have air traffic halted during the operation.

Guardian, you'll secure Jose and keep him safe.

Trojan, have a diversion ready in case we need one.

Merlin and Spider, take out the guards and secure the tower.

Boomer, disarm the booby traps and secure the fence line.

Muskrat, Beaver and Brutus, you have mop up duties. Take out any and all threats.

Squeaker, you have the comms. Make sure to wire the General up also.

I'll have overwatch from the hilltop. I'll take out Manuel Ortiz as soon as he pops his head out. Take them all out except Jose. I want no one left to warn the others. General, have transportation ready when we're done so that we can get the M72s out of there and make a clean getaway. Is everyone set on what your duties are?"

"Roger, Skipper. We got it."

"General, are you good with being with me? You'll have a bird's eye view of everything that goes on from the hilltop."

"Yes. I'm very excited to watch you and your team in action."

"Good. We're glad to have you along with us. We'll have Brutus and Merlin watch the camp until 14:00. Then come back and get some rest and be ready tonight."

"14:00. Roger, Skipper."

"The rest of you get the gear ready and get some rest. We'll be using silenced Remington Model 16 semiautomatic rifles with sub-sonic rounds. No explosions unless absolutely necessary. Understood?"

"Understood, Skipper."

"Boomer, let me know as soon as you get the fence line secure."

"Roger, Skipper."

"I will not be using Jamie on this op. I'll be using a silenced Remington Model 16 semiautomatic rifle just like the rest of you. Quiet is key on this op. I want a clean in and out. Everyone get your jobs done and get some rest."

"If I may ask, what is a Jamie?"

Everyone laughs at this.

"Jamie is what I call my regular sniper rifle. I named it after my father. It's a M40A1 700 Remington."

"If I might be so bold could I see this rifle?"

"Of course, General. I'll not only let you see it, I'll let you shoot it as well."

"I would be very honored."

The guys look at Travis as if he has lost his mind. In 300 missions together, Travis has never let anyone, not anyone, touch his rifle, much less shoot it. Travis looks at the guys with a "when in Rome" look and smiles.

"General, if you will follow me, I'll show you my rifle. Is there somewhere we can shoot it?"

"Yes, we can shoot it out back of the house."

Travis takes the General out back to shoot Jamie. Travis and the General return after some time with the General rubbing his shoulder and laughing about it being sore.

"All right gentlemen, get some rest and we'll assemble here at 02:00."

FIFTY-NINE

Mission Day

Travis and the guys meet up at the appointed time and leave for the mission. They arrive at the camp and Travis and the General take up overwatch on the hilltop and the others go to their appointed posts to get ready.

"Dragonslayer is in the tower watching the dragon. All knights sound off."

"Genius all clear."

"Falcon all clear."

" Guardian all clear."

"Trojan all clear."

"Merlin all clear."

"Spider all clear."

"Boomer all clear."

"Muskrat all clear."

"Beaver all clear."

"Brutus all clear."

"Squeaker all clear."

"Commence Operation Overlord."

The team springs into action. All but Boomer comes in through the back fence. Boomer's clearing the front fence.

"Skipper, fence is all clear."

"Roger that, Boomer."

Travis watches as the team moves inside the camp and starts taking out the members of the group. Just as Guardian goes inside to secure Jose, Travis sees Manuel come out of his tent. Travis takes aim and lets his breath out slowly. He squeezes the trigger and Manuel goes down. He then moves to the guards in the tower and squeezes off two more rounds and the guards go down.

"Tower is clear. Merlin, Spider, get in there and man that machine gun and light."

"Roger that, Skipper."

"Falcon, status?"

"All clear, Skipper."

"Guardian, status?"

"Package is secure."

"Genius, status?"

"Laws are secured."

"Boomer, wire it up. Everyone else mop it up. Time check, 02:45. Good job, gentlemen. Let's get loaded up and ready to roll."

"Roger that, Skipper"

"Boomer, get ready to light it up."

"Ready, Skipper."

"Everyone loaded and ready?"

"Roger, Skipper."

"Boomer, light it up."

As Travis and the team drive off, Boomer lights up the camp. They watch it explode in the rearview mirror as they set off to the General's home.

Travis and the team get up the next morning and leave for the airport. They load Turner's body and the Laws Rockets onto the plane and return to Washington, DC. Travis knows he'll have a hard time feigning remorse at Turner's funeral.

William E. Boone

WILLIAM E. BOONE
PROUDLY PRESENTS
THE NEXT WORK IN THE
TRAVIS BONES SERIES

THE
GOVERNMENT
SILENTLY
WEEPS

A Political Thriller

Written by

William E. Boone

Turn the page for a preview.........

PRELUDE

Director Smith's Office

After the fallout from the whole Senator Baker scandal, Travis and Director Smith sit down and try to decide what to do with the treasure trove of information accumulated on other members of the Senate and Congress. Travis wants to meet with President Carpenter and involve him in the loop of things. Smith thinks they should just turn everything over to the FBI and be done with it.

"Travis, as you know, the CIA is not allowed to perform investigations on United States soil. The only option we have is to turn the investigation over to the FBI and let Director Hughes take the information and run with it."

"There's only one problem with that whole thing, Chuck. That being, we don't know if he or anybody at the FBI has been compromised by Baker's corruption. We need to find out before we turn anything over to him and have it get mysteriously lost. You, better than anybody, know how the FBI is about accidently losing information if it suits them. Hell, how much stuff did they lose about the whole Democratic office break-in bullshit? Why don't we simply meet with President Carpenter and I'll live with whatever he decides."

"How about we take a week and think things over and see what we come up with after that?"

"You won't mind if I spend that time going through the information to see if I can uncover anything do you, Chuck?"

Smith laughs and nods at Travis. "You know I can't stop you when you put your mind to it."

Travis leaves and goes down to the Op's Center. He hates to contact the guys, as he has just given them time off to see their families. He decides to page the guys and let them know what he'll be doing for the next week. He tells them to enjoy their time at home and he'll contact them if he needs them. The only way he'll do that is if he finds anything. He has a nagging suspicion that he'll find something or someone that has been compromised.

Travis starts digging through the information and it doesn't take long for him to find a name that rings a bell. It appears that FBI Assistant Director Joseph Greene has had dealings with Senator Baker. He'll have to investigate this more in depth. If the assistant director is compromised, who else is he going to find? Smith needs to know about this, but Travis need more information about him first. The more Travis digs, the more names he comes up with that are tied back to Baker. By the time Travis finishes going through the information, he has a list of 13 agents plus the assistant director. Travis is convinced that if they give the information to the FBI, they will bury the information or find a way to lose it and the guilty parties will never be brought to justice. Travis has to find a way to get the President involved or convince Smith that they need to handle the investigation themselves. He knows that the CIA isn't allowed to operate within the borders of the United States, but something has to be done to bring these people to justice and stop the corruption brought about by Baker and his cronies.

ONE

Washington, DC

"This is NBC News with a breaking report out of Washington, DC."

"Good evening everyone. This is Cory Stevens for NBC News. We have just been informed the FBI Director Robert Hughes is about to hold a press conference. We are joining the press conference in progress."

"Good evening, everyone. I'm here tonight to announce that four Federal Judges have been arrested and charged with bribery and obstruction in the wake of the William Baker scandal. The FBI will be conducting an investigation. It's possible that some cases tried by these judges will have to be thrown out in regard to these charges. I'll be keeping the public updated as new developments happen. Thank you. I will not be taking questions at this time. I'll be making updated statements later as events unfold in the investigation."

"Well, there you have it. More bad news for the country in the wake of the Senator Baker scandal.

NBC News will be keeping you up to date as the situation unfolds. This is Cory Stevens for NBC News. We now return you to your regularly scheduled programming."

TWO

48 Hours Earlier

Director Smith's Office

Travis meets Chuck at his office to let him know what he has found. Travis has found too many people in the FBI tied to Baker to feel comfortable with handing the investigation over to the FBI.

"Good morning, Chuck. I don't believe you're going to like what I have to tell you. The assistant director and 13 other agents all have ties running back to Baker and his cronies."

"How the Hell can that many people at the FBI be tied to Baker and his people?"

"Baker had half of Capitol Hill on the hook. It didn't surprise me that he had that many people at the FBI on his payroll or at least owing him favors. That's why I wanted to get the President involved. I know we're not supposed to run investigations domestically, but if we turn this over to them, it'll get buried and nothing will get done."

"I have to agree with you on this one. Sit tight and I'll see if I can get President Carpenter on the line."

Smith calls the President and tells him what Travis has found. The President isn't happy about the findings.

"Hell Chuck, it's not like we didn't have enough problems already! How the Hell did he get his hooks in that many people over there? To know that the assistant director is on the hook to him, just boggles my mind."

"I know, Mr. President. I found it hard to believe until Travis showed me the documentation to back it up. If we turn this over to the FBI at this point, nothing will get done and all the information will probably disappear. I'm just glad that the Director himself is not on the hook to these guys."

"I know what you mean, Chuck. I'll make a phone call and get back to you in a few minutes. I have to talk to the Director and see if he has any idea that his guys are involved like this."

"Thank you, Mr. president. I'll be looking for your call and your recommendations."

Travis and Smith continue to go through all the documentation while they wait for the President to call them back. The more Smith reads, the more he is inclined to agree with Travis. The phone rings and Smith answers.

"Hello, Chuck. I've talked to the Director and he had no idea that any of his guys were tied up in this mess. I've set up a meeting for tomorrow at nine am. It will be me, Director Hughes, you and Travis. Be sure to bring the documentation so we can all take a look at it and come up with a plan. I'll see you tomorrow."

"Sounds good to me, Mr. President. I'll see you tomorrow."

William E. Boone lives in the foothills of North Carolina with his wife and dogs. He enjoys spending time with family and friends and cherishes the time spent with his five grandchildren.

William grew up in a small town north of Raleigh and entered the Marine Corps at age 19. He ran classified missions while in the Corps. He draws from his experience and in-depth research to write the Travis Bones series.

William spent over 35 years in the communications world and has vast knowledge of it. He loves the research needed to do this sort of writing.

William has always enjoyed reading and composing stories to share with family and friends. After having open heart surgery, William decided it was time to pursue his passion for writing on a more professional level. That's what brought about the creation of the Travis Bones series. William welcomes you into his mind for a short period to learn the world of Travis Bones. He hopes you enjoy reading it as much as he enjoys writing it for you.

Visit his website at www.williameboone.com to keep up with the latest works for the Travis Bones series. You can also book interviews, book signings and speaking engagements. William loves his fans and enjoys spending time with them discussing his works.

Twitter@WilliamEBoone1

Made in USA - Kendallville, IN
1207134_9781691341498
12.04.2020 2242